CRAZY SWEET

DANGEROUS.

A sheer red silk muscle shirt didn't leave anything to the imagination, especially not the size, the shape, or the delicacy of the black lace bra she was wearing underneath it.

He bought her a lot of black lace.

Her worn denim jeans had silver studs running down the right leg and were so tight, they should have come with a warning label. A small chamois fanny pack was slung around her waist. Pale ostrich-leather cowboy boots covered her feet. Stacked heels, pointed toes, and worn vamps, they'd seen a lot of long days in a dozen Third World hellholes over the last two years—the two years since Red Dog had created herself from a blank slate and a heart hungry for revenge. She was five feet, five inches of pure, unadulterated, ass-kicking girl, and every day she pushed him. She pushed him hard.

Sometimes he wondered if either of them would survive the trip she was on.

"I'd sure take a piece of that," the man at the table continued, his voice hoarse in a way Travis understood only too well—which did nothing to improve his mood.

"Forget it," another guy said. "That one would just as soon gut you as fu—"

Travis reached back, grabbed the last man by the scruff of his collar, and hauled him around until they were face-to-face.

"Don't," he said, very clearly, very succinctly, and very . . . very calmly.

Rising from his bar stool, he pulled the guy's face even closer to his.

"Don't say it. Don't think it."

Fear flashed through the man's eyes, and Travis understood that, too. It had been a hard two years since the night Red Dog had lost her first life and started on her second, and those two years, on the front line with Special Defense Force, a group of black ops warriors based in Denver, Colorado, had changed him. Only one person ever mistook him for anything close to an angel anymore.

Letting go of the man's shirt, he started toward the end of the bar and the woman standing there, waiting for him.

Gillian Pentycote—that had been her name before Dr. Souk, a maniacal physician in the employ of a drug lord, had shot her full of an experimental "truth serum" called XT7 and stolen her memories. By the time Travis and his teammate, Skeeter B. Hart, had gotten to her, there had been nothing left but her screams and four images burned into her brain—only four.

His steps faltered for the barest fraction of a second, less than a heartbeat's worth of pause.

CRAZY
SWEET

Tara
Janzen

A DELL BOOK

CRAZY SWEET
A Dell Book / November 2006

Published by
Bantam Dell
A Division of Random House, Inc.
New York, New York

This is a work of fiction. Names, characters, places, and
incidents either are the product of the author's imagination or
are used fictitiously. Any resemblance to actual persons, living
or dead, events, or locales is entirely coincidental.

Dell is a registered trademark of Random House, Inc., and
the colophon is a trademark of Random House, Inc.

ISBN 978-0-440-24279-6

Printed in the United States of America
Published simultaneously in Canada

www.bantamdell.com

OPM 10 9 8 7 6 5 4 3 2 1

CRAZY
SWEET

CHAPTER

THE ROAR AND RUMBLE of the pipes on the car pulling up outside Beck's Back Alley Bar were unmistakable, headers and the dual exhaust of the bad girl's ride, tuned to perfection and guaranteed to shake glass in four directions. Red Dog was here—back from cheating death one more time.

Travis James let out a heavy breath and knocked back a shot of tequila before he turned to face the front door. He hated to miss her entrance. Watching Red Dog walk into a room was the best floor show in town—in any town.

"Geezus," the guy sitting at the table behind him said when the door opened.

Oh, yeah. She had that effect on him, too—all the time, every time.

He chased the tequila with a swallow of beer and let his gaze drop down the length of her body. She was so bad, she was good. Good like seven-dollar-a-shot mescal, and exquisitely, classy bad.

Dangerous.

A sheer red silk muscle shirt didn't leave anything to the imagination, especially not the size, the shape, or the delicacy of the black lace bra she was wearing underneath it.

He bought her a lot of black lace.

Her worn denim jeans had silver studs running down the right leg and were so tight, they should have come with a warning label. A small chamois fanny pack was slung around her waist. Pale ostrich-leather cowboy boots covered her feet. Stacked heels, pointed toes, and worn vamps, they'd seen a lot of long days in a dozen Third World hellholes over the last two years—the two years since Red Dog had created herself from a blank slate and a heart hungry for revenge. She was five feet, five inches of pure, unadulterated, ass-kicking girl, and every day she pushed him. She pushed him hard.

Sometimes he wondered if either of them would survive the trip she was on.

"I'd sure take a piece of that," the man at the table continued, his voice hoarse in a way Travis understood only too well—which did nothing to improve his mood.

"Forget it," another guy said. "That one would just as soon gut you as fu—"

Travis reached back, grabbed the last man by the scruff of his collar, and hauled him around until they were face-to-face.

"Don't," he said, very clearly, very succinctly, and very . . . very calmly.

Rising from his bar stool, he pulled the guy's face even closer to his.

"Don't say it. Don't think it."

Fear flashed through the man's eyes, and Travis understood that, too. It had been a hard two years since the night Red Dog had lost her first life and started on her second, and those two years, on the front line with Special Defense Force, a group of black ops warriors based in Denver, Colorado, had changed Travis. Only one person ever mistook him for anything close to an angel anymore.

Letting go of the man's shirt, he started toward the end of the bar and the woman standing there, waiting for him.

Gillian Pentycote—that had been her name before Dr. Souk, a maniacal physician in the employ of a drug lord, had shot her full of an experimental "truth serum" called XT7 and stolen her memories. By the time Travis and his teammate, Skeeter B.

Hart, had gotten to her, there had been nothing left but her screams and four images burned into her brain—only four.

His steps faltered for the barest fraction of a second, less than a heartbeat's worth of pause.

Walking on, he wiped the back of his hand across his mouth.

The faces of the two men who had tortured her were half of her shortchanged memory bank: Dr. Souk, his dark and dirty hair, wire-rimmed glasses, and openmouthed death shock when Travis's .45 caliber slug had punched a hole in his chest—a memory Travis wouldn't wish on anybody, let alone a woman, even one with Red Dog's resume; and Tony Royce, the CIA agent gone bad, who had set her up for the pain she'd endured strapped into Souk's dental chair.

Tony Royce, whose face Skeeter had cut open with her knife.

Tony Royce, who had escaped that night and disappeared.

Tony Royce, whom Red Dog hunted with a vengeance born of desperation.

It was her desperation that kept Travis always on edge. She was a gun for hire. She went to bad places and did bad things to bad people, and so far, every time, she'd come back to him. But time was running out. He felt it with each passing day, with each mission she survived. He felt it when they worked together, and he felt it when she went out without him, like she had this time.

"You're late," he said, coming to a stop in front of her and taking hold of her arm. Contact, that's what he needed, physical contact.

"Things came up." The huskiness of her voice told him how tired she was, how run-down.

"Four *days* late." He tried to keep the frustration out of his words, and failed.

"El Salvador is kind of a long ways away." She ran her hand back through her short auburn hair, sending a little more of it sticking up on end. She was a wild girl, the wildest.

El Salvador?

"The mission was in Panama," he said, his jaw tight. *Fucking El Salvador?*

"I took a side trip."

Which was the last goddamn thing he wanted to hear, even if he'd already figured that much out. Her "side trips" had only one motivation: Tony Royce.

"What did you find?"

"Nothing. It was a rumor."

And that was a lie. He could tell by the way she avoided meeting his eyes.

He tightened his hold on her. He wanted the truth. He needed to know, but she never gave him what he wanted, and barely gave him what he needed. She had a head full of bits and pieces, and that's all she ever offered of herself—except in bed.

Geezus.

Sex wasn't love, though, and it wasn't trust, and though he didn't know a damn thing about love anymore, and in retrospect doubted if he ever had, he did know about trust—and he wanted hers. It was the only way he could ever keep her safe.

She'd been laying a trapline for Royce since she'd walked out of rehab, and any day, the bastard was going to catch the scent and come after her. It was what she hoped for, what she prayed for, that the man who had stood over Gillian Pentycote and watched her lose her mind would come for the woman she'd become. That Royce would come for Red Dog.

It was all she wanted, and the only thing Travis feared—that Royce would find her somewhere, sometime, someplace when he wasn't by her side. Some goddamn place like El Salvador.

A moment passed. Then she lifted her gaze to his, and looking down into her eyes, he suddenly didn't give a damn if she lied, and he didn't care that she pushed him hard and kept him on edge. Tonight, she was back. She was safe. And even if she didn't know who she was, she knew she was his.

"Take me home, Angel," she whispered, closing

her hand around his shirt and leaning against him, tearing him up and turning him on at the same time. "I'm tired. The Panama deal, it was rough."

Angel. That was her third memory, the name she remembered him by. And lastly, she remembered his face, the face of the man who had made love to her that night, before she'd been abducted, before Souk had injected her—before her life had taken a sharp left into hell.

Take me home.

It was the one thing he could do: take her home . . . and take her.

Still holding on to her arm, he turned her around and started for the door, but she stopped after two strides and looked up at him again.

"Don't you have something for me?" she asked.

She always asked, and he *always* had something for her, whatever she wanted.

But he knew what she meant, and he reached into the front pocket of his jeans. Inch by soft silky inch, he pulled out a scrap of black lace.

"A new bra?" She reached for the small piece of lingerie.

"No, baby. Panties." Super-short, boy-cut underwear, the bit of stretchy lace would sit low on her hips and curve up over her ass, leaving a lot of bare bottom for his profound personal enjoyment—and she thought he bought the stuff for her.

Yeah. Right.

With a smile that damn near slayed him on the spot, she took the underwear and shoved it into her own pocket. "I hope they fit."

They fit. He knew the shape of her body better than he knew his own. Their relationship was very "hands on"—his hands on her, and his hands were the only hands on her, ever. Nobody touched Red Dog except him, not even her mother, which broke the woman's heart, the way everything that had happened to her daughter broke Lydia Shore's heart—especially what her daughter had become.

Mercenary. Contractor. Whoever wrote the paycheck, the job was the same. Two days ago in Thailand, he'd heard the word "assassin" connected to her name, along with a price tag that guaranteed Gillian could provide for herself in whatever manner she chose, for as long as she chose to stay in business.

Assassin? Maybe. Unsung hero—just as likely, considering the kind of men Red Dog took down. It was all a matter of semantics and point of view. There wasn't an SDF operator at Steele Street or a combat soldier in the employ of Uncle Sam who hadn't been tagged an assassin by somebody, somewhere. But Red Dog wasn't really an SDF operator, and she certainly wasn't a U.S. soldier. By most standards, she was unemployable, except in the niche Christian Hawkins and Kid Chaos had trained her to fill.

Sometimes, lately, Travis wondered what in the hell Superman and the Boy Wonder had been thinking, but in the beginning, he'd understood what they were doing only too well. She'd been so lost when she'd first come out of her drug-induced coma, so detached. Hawkins had given her something to hold on to: physical training. Her memories were gone, but she was alive. Her body worked, so Superman had worked her hard, made her fight for herself. Then Hawkins had given her to Kid, and Kid had taken her to a remote Department of Defense training camp high in the Rocky Mountains and taught her how to fight for a living.

Panama had been the seventh job she'd taken without Travis—and as far as he was concerned, it was her last. He was finished with not knowing where in the hell she was, or what in the hell she was doing, or even if she was alive. Nothing felt right, not when she was out and he wasn't there to watch her back.

And then to disappear off the face of the earth—well, hell, that was way more than he had the strength to endure anymore, especially when he was in goddamn Thailand, thousands of miles away.

It was General Grant himself who had author-
ized her to work with C. Smith Rydell, the newest
member of the SDF team, in Panama, and it was
Grant who had called Hawkins and congratulated
him on his protégé's latest successful mission. So if
everything had gone so well and the job was finished, Hawkins had wondered, why in the hell
hadn't she come home?

Travis had wondered the same damn thing
when Superman had called him, and by nightfall
he'd been on a plane.

Fuck. Four days—that's how much time had
passed between when she'd left Smith in Panama
City and when she'd checked in with Hawkins and
told him she was headed back to Denver. Four
days: plenty of time for her to have gotten herself
into more trouble than she could handle.

Going to El Salvador. Alone.

He needed to clip her wings, lock her in, tie her
down, whatever it took to keep her in his sight.
The DOD didn't give a damn if she lived or died,
as long as she accomplished her missions, but he
cared—too much.

Sliding his hand to her waist, he started toward
the door again. Beck's Back Alley Bar was in an industrial section of north Denver called Commerce
City, tucked between the refineries and the factories on a strip of street eight blocks west of the

Steele Street Commerce City garage. The garage was an annex to the SDF headquarters in LoDo, the only place in Denver with enough security to suit Travis. Hawkins and the boss of SDF, Dylan Hart, had both offered Gillian one of the upper-floor lofts at Steele Street, but the bad girl wasn't looking for security. She didn't want to be hard to find.

Quite the opposite, and it unnerved the hell out of Travis.

"Give me your keys," he said, opening the door for her and glancing toward the 1967 Pontiac GTO parked in front of the bar. Chrome bumpers, bright trim, and six coats of wet-sanded and polished Signet Gold paint gleamed in the summer sunlight of late afternoon. Coralie was her name, Corinna's sister, and with a 360-horse Ram Air 400 under the hood and a four-speed Muncie on deck, she was as bad as the girl who drove her.

He unlocked the car and handed Gillian in before giving back the keys.

"Straight home," he said, making himself absolutely clear.

"Straight." She nodded, sliding into the butter-soft, custom black leather interior.

"Five minutes." It shouldn't take more, not in Coralie, but he never took anything for granted, not with her.

"Two, if we blow the lights," she said, glancing back up at him.

He grinned and shook his head.

"Not on my watch, babe. Five minutes." He turned and headed toward his Jeep.

Behind him, he heard the GTO start up, the deep rumbling purr of her engine and headers echoing in the alley. Coralie had been a gift to Gillian from Dylan, a classic piece of muscle for the woman they'd all been too late to save. The boss had been the target that night, not a sweet-faced, tousle-haired thirty-three-year-old "wannabe" assistant trying to work her way up the ladder in General Grant's office.

She still had a sweet face, sweetly exotic, except when seen from the muzzle end of an SR-25 rifle or her TC Contender pistol. "Sweet" wasn't the word that came to mind in those situations. She had a Glock 17 long slide reworked to a .40 Smith & Wesson in her fanny pack, and a seven-inch Recon Tanto sheathed in her boot—razor sharp. He'd seen the clip of her folding knife hooked over her pants pocket. He knew if he looked, he'd find a 12-gauge tactical shotgun under Coralie's front seat, a flat black beauty called "Nightshade" that Gillian kept loaded with double-ought buck and rifled slugs. Her breaching loads were in the glove box.

Two knives, a shotgun, and a semiautomatic pistol, just to visit the neighborhood bar. *Nobody* touched Red Dog. No man could get a hand on her, not on his own.

But Royce wouldn't be alone when he came. The ex-CIA agent had recruited a dozen of the most notorious mercenaries operating on the international scene to headline his underworld organization, every one of them a hardened criminal, the kind of men who would kill each other for the right price. The DOD had dubbed them the Damn Dirty Dozen, and they were on wanted lists from London to Laos, their reputations the stuff of people's nightmares.

Travis knew each of them by name, face, and rap sheet. He'd made it his business to know, and if Tony Royce had moved into El Salvador, they'd been there with him—with Red Dog not nearly far enough behind.

She was going to get herself killed, unless he got to Royce before Royce got to her—so he hunted. He followed the mercs, he followed the money, he followed the deals, always looking for the man who stayed hidden behind it all: Tony Royce. Two weeks ago, a source had pinpointed the former U.S. government agent in Bangkok, cutting a deal on illegal psychopharmaceuticals, the kind of drugs that Dr. Souk had used on Gillian. But when he and Kid had gotten to Thailand the trail had been cold, and it had stayed cold—until now.

She was wrong. El Salvador wasn't far away, not at all. Travis could be there in a matter of hours.

Rounding the tail end of his Jeep, he glanced down at the license plate—SRCHN4U—and a brief smile twisted his lips. He'd spent his whole life searching for something—the astral plane, the perfect meditation, the solutions to other people's problems—but nothing had ever compelled him with more deadly and serious intent than the search for the man who had destroyed Gillian Pentycote's mind and turned her into a highly professional, highly paid, covert operator who knew herself only by the code name Red Dog.

CHAPTER

2

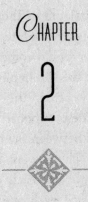

GILLIAN PUSHED OPEN the heavy iron door leading to her loft above the Commerce City garage and dropped her duffel bag just inside on the floor. There were locks on the door, but she didn't bother to use them. Her name painted in red across the dull gray metal was enough to keep out the local riffraff. Nobody in Commerce City wanted to get on Red Dog's bad side. She was a little too sketchy, a little too mysterious, with a street rep for having more firepower than anyone could possibly need merely for self-defense. The reputation was well earned; the rumors told were true, and every gangster on the north side knew it. They also knew she had friends, friends like Christian Hawkins and Creed Rivera, and in Denver,

Colorado, it only took one of those names to guarantee her security—her absolute, total security.

Only an outsider would come for her here, and that's exactly what she was hoping for.

Striding quickly across the large room, she headed for a Japanese cupboard sitting by itself against the far wall between the open kitchen area and the fireplace. There were a hundred small drawers in the cupboard, each one with a *kanji* carved into its surface, each one of them wishing her something nice: long life, good fortune, health, wealth, happiness, peace, joy, comfort, love, compassion, mercy, justice, and on, and on, and on, all the good things.

Lydia Shore had given her the cupboard, brought it back with her from a recent trip to Osaka. Lydia and her husband, Alan, were nice. Gillian liked them, even if their connection to her was nothing more than a confusing blur. Regardless, she'd instantly been taken with the woman's gift, with the cupboard's warm, worn wooden drawers, with each one's intricately cast bronze handle, with the ancientness of the piece. Two hundred and fifty years old, Lydia had told her, so old, so sturdy, and yet with a softness about it.

Gillian liked soft things, insisted on them. The only hard things she allowed in her life were her weapons—and her weapons were very hard. Sharp. Clean. Loaded. Lethal.

Running her fingers over the drawers, she stopped at number forty-three, Tony Royce's drawer, and pulled it open. A small pile of newspaper clippings were tucked inside, each with the paper's name, place of publication, and date. She took the latest addition out of her back pocket and laid it on top of the others: *La Prensa; San Luis, El Salvador;* and yesterday's date.

She'd been too late to get him in her sights, missed him by two days, but he'd been there in his new Central American lair, the monster who hid in the back of her brain and lunged out of the muddy darkness of her memories to sabotage her.

She'd left him a message. One he wouldn't miss. One he couldn't resist. This time, he would come for her.

She was counting on it with everything she had.

Royce wasn't the only monster who haunted the dark recesses of her mind, but the other man, Dr. Souk, was dead. She knew it deep down in her gut. Every time she saw the sallow-faced doctor standing next to Royce, leaning over her with a syringe in his hand, she also saw a bullet rip through his chest.

It was a comfort.

Such a comfort to know he was dead, no matter how much blood filled the image.

And yes, she knew she was a strange woman not to mind Souk's blood, but the white room had been splattered with lots of blood by then. Even stranger, sometimes, if she moved slowly enough in her dreams, carefully enough, she could turn her head and follow the path of the bullet back through the air—back across the endless sea of pain to where it had come from, back to the angel, to the gun in his hand, to the cold calculation in his eyes and the hard, brutally calm set of his face.

And sometimes she was able to keep going back—back out the door, out of the building, back through the woods... *back, back, back... before*—

She let out a soft curse and closed the drawer. She never got out of the woods. Never.

Never got away from the men who had hauled her down the path, dragging her toward the lights and the building in the trees, into the white room. Always there was so much... *white*.

Shit! A spasm of pain shot down her arm, instantly drawing every tendon tight, automatically clenching her hand into a fist—her gun hand. *Goddamn.* Dreams, memories, and the white room were no place for her to go when she'd been pushing herself so hard, when she was tired.

Another spasm ripped through her, tightening her arm even more, and she gasped.

It hurt. It always hurt, but she didn't panic. She never panicked over reality and the goddamn aftereffects of being injected with XT7. The stuff was never going to go away, not completely, not ever. She'd been the Lab Rat of the Year for two years running over at Walter Reed. There was a doctor there, Dr. Brandt, who tested her every month. He was brilliant, insightful, and kind, too kind not to give her hope.

But she knew how the cards lay, so she dealt with the pain, and saved her panic for Royce. That boy was going away someday, with one of her match-grade bullets through his head. Sometimes he ate her alive with panic and terror, his scream of pain twisting his face and echoing in her ear, blood flowing from a gash that started above his eyebrow and went all the way to his jaw.

Skeeter had done that to him, caught him with her knife and laid his face open.

Taking a breath, she shifted her attention from her rigid tendons to her pulse, and with every beat of her heart, she let space and softness flow down through her veins. Her body had been such a wreck until Superman had made her strong and Angel had taught her how to breathe.

The seconds passed with her heartbeat, one

after the other. When the door to the loft swung open, she looked toward it.

No panic. She knew who it was. Angel had been on her tail all the way from Beck's, driving the crappy old Jeep Skeeter barely kept together for him. The Jeep spent more time at 738 Steele Street than he did.

"Hey," she said.

"Hey." His gaze immediately went to her arm, but he didn't say anything. He knew what she needed, and it wasn't talk, not when it came to her arm.

She watched him cross the room, her gaze following every step he took, following the ease with which he unbuttoned his shirt and shrugged out of it. With a small toss, the shirt ended up in a pile next to her bed, a built-up pallet on the floor covered with layer upon layer of soft blankets, cotton sheets, silk pillows, chenille throws, and a gossamer canopy in rich shades of green and gold.

His shoulder holster came off next, and he set it and his pistol on a table by the bed. Then he reached back and pulled his T-shirt off over the top of his head. With another toss, it landed on top of his collared shirt.

Angel...his hands went to his belt, and her heart started to slow, the softness in her veins to deepen.

He was beautiful, exquisitely so, his dark blond hair tied in a ponytail at the nape of his neck, his face more rugged than it once had been, his body more starkly chiseled than in most of the paintings she'd seen of him, angel paintings done by his friend Nikki Chronopolous.

She owned two of Nikki's paintings: an ascending angel, where he appeared almost transparent, he was so shot through with golden light, and a descending angel. Dark and tortured, lost and falling, the descending angel reminded her of what she'd been when she'd first woken up into her nightmare.

Another spasm of pain rolled down the length of her arm, less severe, but enough to pull a soft groan out of her.

He turned, still unbuckling his belt, and cocked his head toward an open arch in the wall on the other side of the bed. "You want to do this?"

She nodded silently. He knew she did.

His hands moved to the top button on the fly of his jeans, and when she didn't move, he spoke again.

"Do you need help?" His fingers moved down to the second button, then the next one.

Yes. Oh, yes. Her gaze followed the last button as he slipped it open. She watched the slide of his pants down his legs, watched him toe out of his

boots and step out of his jeans, and leave everything, including his boxers, in a pile on the floor.

He was so unabashed, years younger than she,
and so still, even in motion. She loved his still-
ness, the calm ease with which he moved and
thought, and he thought a lot, about everything.
He was highly intelligent, highly educated, com-
passionate, kind, philosophical, generous, and absolutely deadly—lethally skilled.

And until Royce came for her, he was still hers.
A couple more weeks at the best, only days if her
plan had worked.

She knew the cost of what she'd done in San
Luis. Part of it was going to be leaving Angel behind. He deserved better than a life on the run—
and once she killed Royce, she would be running
hard until the day she died.

He started toward her, naked, pulling the band
off his ponytail and dragging both of his hands
back through his hair . . . *Angel*.

Her pulse picked up, a slow hum of desire replacing her pain. He was so good for her.

She knew he hunted Royce and planned on
killing him if the chance arose, but that would
never do. The monster was hers to slay. There was
no other way.

Angel . . . angel . . . angel—he was everything she'd
clung to so desperately as the pain and the drugs

had slowly eaten away at her memories, destroying the years of her life and making them disappear. It was his image she'd conjured against the agony, his name she'd formed in her mind to combat the fear.

He touched a switch on the wall next to the cupboard, and warm, subdued light filled the arch behind the bed, revealing a glassed-in shower, an open shelf full of soft, peach-colored towels, and the curved recesses of a large, jetted bathtub.

Circling behind her, he slid his hands around her waist and took hold of the bottom of her shirt. He had strong, large hands, sure hands.

"Lift up," he said.

She did the best she could, and he gently pulled her shirt off over her head. Another easy toss landed the soft pile of sheer red silk on top of his T-shirt. The black lace bra came off next, and his hands came around to cup her breasts.

With a sigh, she relaxed back against his naked chest, resting her head in the crook of his shoulder, letting him play with her. His mouth came down on the side of her neck, his tongue laving her skin, his fingertips brushing across her nipples, and she relaxed even more deeply against him.

He was so good for her.

He moved his hands to the top of her zipper, and with her help, they got her out of her jeans and boots. Then he did a panty switch on her, slipping the new scrap of boy-cut lace up her legs and over her hips: a perfect fit.

His gifts always made her feel so sweet—and so sweetly bad.

She arched up on her toes, the pain in her arm drifting away as his hand slid around her waist and down between her legs, under the lace. He cupped her there, pulling her close against him, against his arousal.

A groan slipped free from her mouth. God, how she loved him, how she loved this—being close, knowing they'd soon be even closer, with him deep inside her.

He parted her with his fingers, touched her, and a wave of melting pleasure washed through her, leaving a slight tremor in its wake.

He understood.

"Come on, baby." He pulled his hand out from between her legs and swung her up into his arms, holding her close.

A light dusting of dark brown hair covered his chest, and she ran her fingers through it. He grinned at her and tightened his hold.

She loved his smile, the warmth of it, the ingenuousness of it. When he smiled, the hardness of the last two years slipped away from him, and he looked more like the angels in the paintings, more like what he'd been before the night their lives had changed. He'd been her salvation that night, and her redemption ever since. Only the direst circumstances could ever take her from his side, could make her walk away and never look back—and she wouldn't be looking back. Not once. She'd sworn it.

He carried her straight into the shower, panties and all, and started a warm stream of water pouring over them—and then he started in on her with his hands. "Sexual imprinting" he called his massage technique, a hands-on method of physical and emotional therapy he'd refined over the last two years to be specifically sexual, and specifically for her.

She felt his palms and his fingers moving over her, working on her, easing the tension from the muscles in her back and shoulders. She felt his strength and the skill of his hands as the water grew warmer and fogged the glass, blocking out the rest of the world.

And she felt the heat of his touch, the softness of the creamy soap he was smoothing over her.

He would find love again. He'd been made for love—and tonight he'd been made for loving her. Turning in his arms, she slid her hands around his neck, through his hair, and stretched up to meet his kiss.

CHAPTER 3

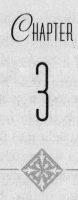

C. SMITH RYDELL sat outside a cantina across from the Hotel Palacio in San Luis, El Salvador, drinking a beer, watching the street, and wondering if it was possible for the town to get through the night without something exploding or going up in flames.

Probably not, he decided. According to the local newspaper, *La Prensa*, there had been two explosions and five car burnings in the last week—and now the weekend had arrived. Things were bound to heat up when the sun went down, and it was sliding fast, sinking into the ocean like it had more sense than to stick around San Luis in the dark.

Hot tropical nights, hot tropical country, hot tropical politics, gangs, drug lords, the disenfranchised remnants of the civil war rallying into a rebel force in the mountains, and him smack dab in the middle of all of it—business as usual, except this round of adventure could be laid squarely at Red Dog's feet. C. Smith Rydell had arrived this morning, almost immediately realized he'd missed her, and spent the rest of the day gathering intel and figuring out just exactly how much trouble she'd gotten herself into since they'd wrapped their Panama mission.

Plenty, and then some, and as soon as he figured out why his secure cell wasn't working with the local system, he needed to let the boys at Steele Street know. The other option, going through the hassle of opening a Salvadoran cell account, was way at the bottom of his list, especially since he was heading back to the States first thing in the morning. So for now, C. Smith Rydell was drinking his beer and watching the street. He was especially watching the people on the street, and as of two minutes ago, most especially watching the tawny-haired blonde in the tight white halter dress with the red polka dots, little matching jacket, and white bow-tied spike heels with the two-inch platforms, which brought her all the way up to about five feet four—maybe. She was carrying a straw tote bag that was almost as big as she was, had hoop earrings the size of saucers and white designer sunglasses so big they barely perched on her nose. She also had, unbelievably, three tiny red polka-dot bows scooping up all that tawny blond hair into an elegant, if slightly mussed, French twist, which was more appropriate than a person might imagine, because she looked like something straight out of a brochure for the French Riviera. She looked like candy, sure, but expensive candy. The polish on her toes matched the polka dots, the flowers on her tote matched her toes, and her lipstick matched both.

C. Smith Rydell took another slow sip of beer, waiting, his gaze following her through his Ray-Bans. Certain laws of physics all but guaranteed that something was going to fall out of a dress that tight, and so help him God, he didn't want to miss anything when it happened. The halter top, in particular, was giving him whiplash, even though he'd barely moved a muscle since he'd seen her.

Candy. Eye candy, sex candy, melt-in-your-mouth-and-come-back-for-more candy—all of it wrapped in polka dots and a bolero-style jacket that didn't quite make the dress modest. She looked like she was more trouble than she was worth, but sometimes that sort of reasoning didn't really register in a guy's brain.

Smith wondered, idly, if it was registering in his. She was definitely in the wrong place at the wrong time. He knew that much. As long as she'd kept moving, she'd been almost okay, but she'd stopped to sort through some street vendor's cart of junk in front of the Palacio, and it was setting him on edge. She was one full block off the beaten path, the path the tourists took from one almost-brand-name hotel to the next, with stops in between for a couple of cute boutiques, cute cafés, and a light sprinkling of franchised restaurants. "Fledgling" was the word most analysts used to describe El Salvador's tourist industry, and she was one full block and a bit away from it.

She'd slipped into decrepit-hotel-and-locals'-bar land, which was only a block from El Salvadoran barrio land, which was no place for a curvy blonde in a tight dress and platform heels—especially when his room on the third floor of the old Palacio had been chosen specifically for the view it gave him into the courtyard of Tony Royce's backstreet villa.

Yessirree, the whole friggin' town of San Luis was crawling with bad guys—real bad guys—and there wasn't a one of them who wouldn't want a piece of what he was looking at.

She needed a keeper, and women who looked like that usually had one who didn't let them too far out of their sight. So where was hers? There had to be some rich old guy tagging along behind her somewhere, but Smith wasn't taking the time to look for the lucky bastard. He didn't dare.

He took another swallow of beer without taking his eyes off her. He didn't care what the hell was in the vendor's cart, it wasn't worth the trouble she was going to find if she didn't get her butt back to her oceanfront hotel.

The sooner the better. Smith wasn't the only one who had noticed her. She was starting to draw looks from every direction, and it wouldn't be too long before the guards patrolling Tony Royce's gated mausoleum of a house checked the street and noticed her, too.

He had his bottle of beer halfway to his mouth, when the fat lady sang. Almost on cue, the blonde's time was up. Royce's men had spotted her. Two of them were coming through the big iron gate that fronted the street, one of them visibly packing a pistol, both of them heading straight for her, looking damned serious and like maybe they wanted to have some fun—bad fun.

Dammit.

Smith pushed himself out of his chair and abandoned his beer.

Saving damsels in distress wasn't anywhere in his mission statement or his job description, but here he was, moseying across the street, getting ready to put himself between the bad guys and the cupcake.

It occurred to him that with his blue parrot shirt, baggy cargo pants, a day's worth of beard, and scruffy haircut, he might not exactly look like a hero coming to her rescue, but he'd play that part by ear. All he needed to do was get her moving in the right direction, which was west. Due west. Back to the ocean and the one paved street in San Luis.

To that end, he speeded up his gait. She'd lifted a leather-wrapped bundle of something or another out of the cart and was giving it a once-over. With a hasty move, the vendor shoved the bundle toward her tote. She resisted for a second, but then he put a wooden crucifix on top of the bundle, and both items went into her bag. After another second's hesitation, she pulled out some cash and handed it over.

Smith swore softly under his breath. She was going to get herself royally harassed at the least, or royally manhandled, or even worse, all for a bundle of junk and a wooden crucifix.

Out of the corner of his eye, he caught sight of a third man coming out of the villa's gate with a sub-gun slung over his shoulder—and wasn't that just perfect?

"Arturo!" one of the first men called out.

Smith gave the guy a quick glance, saw him gesture down the street; when Smith looked, there was guy number four, carrying an AR15 carbine, crossing over in front of a battered old Ford pickup and heading for the woman and the Palacio.

If the situation had been perfect before, now it was absolutely perfect—him, the cupcake, and four of Tony Royce's handpicked, well-armed assholes.

He looked back to the cart—and she was gone. The cupcake in polka dots. Completely disappeared.

How in the hell, he wondered, had she moved so fast in platform heels, and where in the hell had she gone?

There was only one answer to the second question. She'd been standing in front of the Hotel Palacio's oversized wooden doors, and the only place she could have disappeared that quickly was through them.

Well, that had to be a bit of a shock to her. The Palacio was a fortress, with solid masonry walls and thick hardwood floors and doors, but the hotel was also as flea-bitten as they came, with fading paint and chipping plaster, a nicked and scarred reception counter, and a pair of bullet craters in the wall at the bottom of the staircase. There was no elevator in the Palacio. The place was eighty years old if it was a day, a three-story hollow rectangle with interior verandas running around each of the floors, overlooking a lush, overgrown courtyard. Smith had taken the third-floor suite on the southeast corner of the building and had spent most of the day shrouded in the dim light behind his balcony window, looking through a compact 20-power spotting scope pointed at Royce's villa.

He'd seen plenty, especially the hit-ups Red Dog had spray-painted on Royce's stucco walls and the fallout of her handiwork. There were four tags visible from the courtyard, and two guys doing their best to wash them off or paint over them, neither of which was working. *Red Dog 303* in big red letters and numbers had been bleeding through every coat of paint the men had put on today. She'd made Royce's villa look like a crack house in East L.A.

She had to have loved that, tagging the bastard without getting caught by his security system or his guards, but Smith knew Gillian, and he knew the coup de grâce had been the half-million-dollar cocaine deal she'd screwed up between Royce and Mara Plata, a Central American gang whose business specialties included extortion and drug-trafficking. He'd gotten the news about the pooched deal from his old friends at the DEA Country Office in Panama City two days ago. They hadn't been any too happy to have the case they were trying to build against Royce blown for them, and they were going to be even unhappier when he told them who had been involved. *La cazadora espectral*, the ghostly hunter, she was called in Central America, her reputation made with a hit a year ago on a Guatemalan crime boss who'd been exporting his assassination services to the United States. When Christian Hawkins had called Smith yesterday and asked him to follow up on Red Dog's unauthorized side trip to El Salvador, way too many pieces had fallen into place. Seeing her tag splashed all over Royce's walls had confirmed it all, Superman's worst suspicions and Travis James's biggest fear.

The Mara Plata deal wasn't the only one the other two SDF operators thought Red Dog might have mangled for Royce over the last two years, but Smith could guarantee, no matter what she'd done before, this was the first time she'd actually signed her name and address to the deed. He needed to call Hawkins and tell him to batten down the hatches. It didn't take a decoder ring to figure out what *Red Dog 303* meant, and wherever Royce was, Smith didn't think it would take the bastard too damn long to sic somebody on her tail—somebody mean and out for blood.

The girl loved trouble, beyond a doubt, the kind

of trouble she could dish out, which Smith had a tremendous amount of respect and appreciation for. But this kind of trouble made him wish Hawkins or Travis would lock her up until Tony Royce was either dropped into a bottomless pit in Leavenworth, or dead.

Preferably dead.

The guy was sick in a bad way, especially when it came to women, which made Smith walk a little faster. The cupcake wouldn't last five minutes in Royce's company. Not that Smith had seen Royce around, and given the lax attitude of the guards, leaving the grounds to harass a woman, he doubted if Royce was in residence. The ex-CIA agent had a reputation for brutality that extended beyond his twisted inclinations toward the fairer sex.

Arturo and his gang were mid-street when Smith pushed through the doors of the Palacio— just in time to see a flash of white with red polka dots disappear beyond the first landing of the stair-case.

Geezus. She couldn't possibly be staying at the Palacio. The place was a dump, even by his stan-dards, which he could guarantee were lower than hers.

He cruised by the hotel clerk with a short wave and started up the stairs. Casual, that was him, genetically disinclined to panic under any and all circumstances. Still, he was taking the stairs two at a time.

Behind him, he heard Royce's men entering the lobby, which despite everything, surprised him. Harassing a woman on the street was one thing. Following her into a hotel, even one as run-down as the Palacio, was another.

He cleared the first landing and looked down the length of the second-floor veranda. Palm trees from the overgrown courtyard shielded part of the walkway from view, but he still saw her elegantly mussed French twist, the curve of her hip, and one of her platform heels disappear around the corner of the outside staircase, heading toward the top floor.

What in the hell was she up to, he wondered, and where in the hell was she going? There were only two suites on the southern, top-floor wing of the Palacio, his and the Salvadoran honeymooners' next door to him.

Below him, he heard Royce's men entering the courtyard, and behind him, he heard someone coming up the stairs, fast, which for some damn reason, some damn reason in the *Heroism for Dummies* handbook, meant he had to really put his ass on the line here.

Christ. Climbing onto the rail of the veranda, he grabbed the top-floor railing and swung himself up—and landed smack-dab at her white-platformed, spike-heeled, bow-tied feet.

She gasped and froze like a bunny in the headlights, all five feet and practically nothing of tanned legs, tight dress, dangerous curves, and blond hair.

He decided on the spot that unbeknownst to him all these years, candy-apple-red toenail polish was his favorite—something he might have been inclined to contemplate a little more deeply, except for the shouting coming from the courtyard and the sound of feet pounding up the outside stairs.

"Come on," he said, wrapping one arm around her waist and his other hand around her upper arm, which left her with very little weight on her feet, which he most definitely used to his advantage, hustling her toward the door to his room. He had her inside before she could even begin to protest, let alone struggle. He quickly closed the heavy door, shot the top and bottom dead bolts home as quietly as possible, and pressed his ear to the wood, listening.

And that's when he heard the unmistakable sound of somebody racking a round into the chamber of a semiautomatic pistol—except the sound was coming from behind him, not from out on the veranda.

Fuck.

He didn't move for a couple of seconds, just rested his head against the door and silently swore at himself.

"T-turn around," she said, and he figured that was probably not such a bad idea.

Pushing himself off the door panel, he slowly turned to face her and raised his hands to either side of his body. He had a Sig Sauer .45 in a holster jammed in his pants, riding in the small of his back, under his shirt, and he knew that even with her getting the drop on him, he could take her—but he wasn't going to shoot her, or put her to the floor. Not yet. Not when she still looked like a bunny in the headlights. Not when she was still standing exactly where he had first put her, one step away, instead of gaining some distance before drawing her weapon. Not when her hands were shaking so badly he doubted if she could hit the broad side of a barn even at that distance. And not when she didn't have her finger on the trigger.

Nope, both the girl's hands and all her digits were wrapped around the pistol's grip like duct tape. He wondered if she even knew there was a trigger, and he wondered how anyone who knew so little about how to hold a gun had known how to load one.

"My name is John Roland, and I work for the U.S. State Department." That always sounded good

to Americans in a foreign country. It shouldn't, not
necessarily, but it did—and her voice had definitely
tagged her as an American. "Please lower your
gun."

"The—the State Department?" she repeated.

But she didn't lower the gun. Not an inch.

"Yes, ma'am."

"You don't look like you're from the State
Department."

She had a point, a damn good one. He looked
like a merchant marine on a three-day bender, but
he was sticking with his story.

"My office, the embassy where I work, is actually in Panama. I'm here in San Luis on vacation."

"I saw you sitting out in front of the bar across
the street."

Good girl. She'd been paying attention to her
surroundings from behind those big sunglasses. He
was surprised.

"Did you see the men come out of the villa's
gate?"

She nodded, and a blond tendril of hair slipped
free from one of her bows and slid down the side
of her neck to curl in the concave curve above her
collarbone, which was where the plunging V of her
halter top began, which for all the fascination it
held wasn't nearly as riveting as where the V of the
halter top ended.

He took a breath.

"And the fourth guy coming up the street?" he asked. "Did you see him?" The one with the fucking AR15?

She nodded again, and another honey gold strand slipped free to slide across her shoulder. "Th-that's why I came inside the hotel."

He was more than surprised that she'd seen the fourth guy. He was impressed. She'd been standing at the cart, buying junk, and watching the street like a hawk, which really didn't have a damn thing to do with how her skin looked up close, like satin—smooth, soft, and with a subtle sheen that was just a little mind-boggling.

The gun, Smith, he reminded himself. *Keep your eye on the gun.*

"Are you staying here?" He was going to have to take her down and take that damn gun, but he'd really like to do it without breaking her, a consideration that wasn't usually within a hundred miles of his "Things to Do Today" list, not on any day of the week. Up until one minute ago, one hundred percent of the people who had ever pointed a gun at him had been on his "Take Them the Fuck Out" list, Monday through Sunday.

"D-do you have some identification? From the State Department?"

A good question, and no, he didn't, but he went

ahead and carefully lowered his right hand and turned slightly to his left, subtly shifting his weight and giving a damn good impression of someone going for his wallet—and in less than two seconds had her off balance, spun around, and planted solidly against the wall next to the door. Her hands were still gripping the pistol, but he had both of them pinned flat against the plaster above her head, his hip dug into her abdomen, and the V of his right thumb and forefinger around her throat.

Her face had gone instantly pale.

"Let go of the gun," he growled. "Or I'll snap your neck." And that put her way beyond pale into "deathly pale" territory.

He felt her fingers relax, and he pried the weapon free. Then he released his grip on her and stepped away.

Yeah, he thought. It had been a good question, but it had also been one more mistake in a day full of mistakes, starting with her leaving whatever hotel she was staying at, which no way in hell could be the Palacio.

"Where are you staying in San Luis?" he asked, releasing the magazine out of her pistol. Next, he ejected the round she'd loaded into the chamber and let it fall into his hand—a .45, full metal jacket.

When she didn't answer, he glanced up.

Perfect. She was trembling, all over, from the top of her French twist down to her toes, every inch of her—trembling. And suddenly he hoped very much that nothing fell out of her dress.

"What hotel are you at?" he asked again, trying to take a little of the growl out of his voice.

"Th-that's none of your business." She sounded about ready to faint, which was one of the last things he needed.

"It is if you want to get back there in one piece," he said, then checked the magazine. It felt empty, because it was empty.

Sonuvabitch.

"You only had one cartridge?" That didn't make sense. Nobody carried around a semiautomatic pistol with just one cartridge.

"C-cartridge?"

"Bullet," he elaborated. And anyone who didn't know the difference between a bullet and a cartridge shouldn't be carrying anything around.

"There's only one?"

"*Uno.*" He held up the round, and watched her beautiful, lush, candy-apple-red, trembling lips tighten just a bit, in the middle, but he couldn't tell if it was because she was going to cry—*Please, God, anything but that*—or if she was angry.

"I—I paid for three."

Three?

Well, that was just about the stupidest damn thing he'd ever heard.

"Who did you pay?" For three freaking cartridges to put in a seven-round magazine for a semiauto pistol that didn't look like it had been cleaned since World War II.

"The man on the street, the one with the cart."

Oh, geezus.

Suddenly he knew what had been in the bundle, and he knew why Royce's men had come out of the gate, and it wasn't because of a tight white halter dress and honey blond hair.

"Get in the corner, and don't move. Not a muscle, and I mean it," he said, drawing his Sig and gesturing toward the forward corner of the room, where he could keep her in sight, but where she'd be hidden behind the door if it was opened, something he wasn't planning on allowing, but there were four guys out there who might be thinking differently.

Christ. She'd bought a gun off the street, with one friggin' cartridge, which was probably just enough to get her killed, and she'd done it in front of Royce's guards, who would damn well know what kind of business Vendor Man conducted out of his friggin' cart.

He stepped back over to the door to listen.

"I—I don't think you're with the State Department."

"I am," he lied without a second thought. He didn't tell people his business—ever.

"You don't look like anyone I've ever met from the State Department."

That got her a look. "Which State Department, exactly, are we talking about?"

"The one in Washington, D.C."

Geezus.

"I have friends there."

Good. Great.

"Lots of them."

Okay, he wasn't going to run with that, even if she did look like a girl who might have a lot of "friends" anywhere she went.

"And none of them carry a gun."

He wasn't surprised. The job description for State Department pencil pushers didn't usually include disarming beautiful blondes in ratty hotel rooms. No, that thrill-a-minute task was left to guys like him, guys who looked like the kind she'd probably spent her whole life avoiding.

"Y-you do," she added.

Yes, he did, one with plenty of ammo, enough to get him out of the Palacio, if it came to that.

Him and her, too, dammit, if it came to that.

The woman really did need a keeper. It wasn't

going to be him, oh, hell no, but he could at least get her off Tony Royce's street and back over to where the *turistas* played.

"Y-you look like you know what you're doing. With the gun, I mean."

He did, but he sure as hell didn't like this particular turn of the conversation, no more than he liked what he was hearing through the door: the sound of men coming down the veranda.

"You scared me."

He'd meant to scare her.

"And I don't trust you," she said.

Smart girl, he thought, giving her a quick glance where she'd pressed herself into the corner. She was all white swoops and polka-dot curves against the ancient, dull gold paint covering the walls.

"B-but I trust those men out there even less."

A very smart girl, he decided, a very smart and shaking-like-a-leaf-in-a-class-five-hurricane girl who sounded like she was starting to hyperventilate a little.

"I'll p-pay you five hundred d-dollars to be my bodyguard for the next five minutes."

Smith lifted one eyebrow in her direction, then gave her a quick nod and shifted his attention back to the door—and he grinned. He couldn't help himself. Five hundred dollars, and to think he'd been going to save her for free.

CHAPTER

4

"WHAT THE FUCK is this?" Tony Royce asked, looking at the photograph Zane Lowe, his top lieutenant, handed him.

"San Luis." At six feet four and hitting the scales at two-fifty, Zane was a beast—a red-haired beast with a brain.

Royce looked at the picture again, more closely, and felt his jaw lock.

"This is my fucking house?" The windows of his suite at the MGM Grand in Las Vegas overlooked the whole glitzy, overlit, goddamn city—but his gaze was glued to the photograph that Zane had just printed off the computer, a close-up shot of a stucco wall with the number three written on it in red paint.

He'd seen that color of red paint before, four separate times, and every time he'd seen it, bad fucking news had followed. This time, the bad news had arrived first. The goddamn Mara Plata deal he'd been working had been one big goddamn waste of time. The piss ants had leaked the deal.

Now he knew why.

"Yes, sir," Zane said. "The photographs were taken this morning."

"And Manuel just decided to send them now?"

"Yes, sir."

Sir. That was goddamn right. He may have recruited his slag heap of operators out of the gutter, but by God, they either called him sir, or he called them out.

Zane handed him another photo, a long shot, and the full extent of the damage to his million-dollar property and the solution to a whole lot of his problems over the last two years suddenly became crystal clear.

"The stupid bitch."

"Yes, sir."

He glanced at Zane and found his beast grinning.

Zane had problems, psychological problems, but nothing that interfered with his job. Quite the contrary. Sadism was one of Royce's preferred qualities in a job applicant. Not that any of his men had applied. Hell, no. He'd searched each one of them out and offered them the opportunity of a lifetime, to be part of an elite team of international drug-runners with the connections to broker deals and deliver smack from one corner of the earth to another, seamlessly, flawlessly, and by the hundreds of kilograms. Royce was the middleman to the middlemen, with the added bonus of offering a cartel-connected cocaine pipeline into the world's most lucrative markets, and supplying a full line of special-use, high-tech pharmaceuticals guaranteed to blow the head off anybody unlucky enough to end up on the wrong end of one of his needles, a niche market he filled through his private medical staff in Thailand.

Other people could fight for justice, freedom, and the right to vote. He knew what the world wanted. The whole goddamn world wanted to get high, with or without a side order of democracy.

Bangkok, Hong Kong, Islamabad, Vientiane, Rangoon, and Bogotá, he'd known where to find his men, all American expatriates, all floating in black money, all connected to the global, underground economy of illicit drugs and mayhem for hire.

He looked back at the photograph, looked at it through his one pale blue eye. The other had been cut out, sliced right out of his fucking head by a blond bitch with a big knife. Skeeter Bang was still at the top of his hit list, but right under her was the bitch who called herself Red Dog.

The first three times she'd fucked with him, the only thing she'd written in her goddamn red paint was his name, Royce. That was all, just Royce, which had gotten him nothing except pissed off. Two months ago, though, in Uzbekistan, she'd given him "Red Dog," and it hadn't taken him too damn long to find out the only Red Dog on the planet with the skills to screw up one of his deals was a shadowy figure with an attitude. A woman, more than one source had decided when pressed, a woman with a badass Knight SR-25, and both she and the rifle were for sale to the highest bidder on a job-by-job basis—which still had not explained why she was on his ass and on his deals.

But he had a feeling it was all going to become clear real damn soon. She was baiting him, the fool, and he was only too happy to bite.

She'd ruined the paint on his Mercedes in Miami with her goddamn paint and screwed a million-dollar cocaine deal in the process. In Uzbekistan, she'd gotten to Gul Rashid, a warlord he'd been doing business with since the beginning of his now defunct career with the CIA, and some-how gotten Rashid to back out of delivering the ton of Afghan opium Royce had promised to a buyer in Marseille. Then she'd had the balls to leave her calling card in red paint on the sheets in his hotel room: *Red Dog*.

Now she'd gone the extra step. *Red Dog 303*—that's what she'd painted on his million-dollar villa last night, right on the goddamn walls.

He hated women.

And this one, this goddamn Red Dog, he was starting to hate her worst of all.

He stared at the photograph and knew Las Vegas was going to have to wait. She'd pushed him too far.

"Where is area code three-oh-three?" he asked.

"Denver, Colorado," Zane said.

Denver?

Jesus. He looked up from the photograph and pinned Zane with his steely, pale-eyed gaze.

"You know who's in Denver." Goddamn Skeeter Bang and her goddamn husband, Dylan Hart, and their whole goddamn crew of Special Defense Force operators—especially Christian Hawkins, the one they called Superman. *Shit.*

"SDF," Zane confirmed.

"Get on it," Royce ordered. "If it's Bang, I'm dropping a bomb on seven thirty-eight Steele Street."

"And if it's not?" Zane asked.

"Then it's some new bitch they've got on board.

No one of that caliber is working out of Denver without Hart and Hawkins knowing about it. Pull up everything you can find on SDF, including their stringers. We're heading to Denver."

Red Dog 303—the skanky bitch was just begging to be taken out.

After another long moment of staring at the picture, Royce decided he could do a little better than that, even. It had been a while since he'd had some fun. He was due.

He was overdue.

With just a little extra effort, instead of a nice clean hit, he could give her something special. He never went anywhere without a few of his Thai goodies—and while she was screaming her brains out, he could have her sliced and diced.

Zane was the master.

CHAPTER

5

TRAVIS SMOOTHED Gillian's hair back off her face, his fingers sliding through the wet auburn strands, his palms cupping the sides of her head. Her face was tilted toward his, waiting for his kiss. Water from the shower sluiced over them.

He loved her like this—naked, and warm, and safely in his arms.

He lowered his mouth to hers and felt her tongue slip inside. God, she was always so hot, so ready. She never just kissed. She moved into him, dark and sweet, pressing against him in a way that instantly went to his groin.

It was crazy to love a woman who didn't know her own name. He'd seen the blankness that some-times came into her eyes, and the flash of fear that always followed. It scared her, those moments when she became unmoored, far more so than when her arm locked up. She was so tough, so deadly when she needed to be deadly, and yet she was too damn fragile for the job. He'd seen it happen only once while she was working, when she'd gotten "lost" for a brief space of time and failed to pull the trigger when she'd needed to, but once had been more than enough for him. She'd survived, but that failure should have gotten her permanently deactivated, and if she'd been a full-time member of SDF or any other government service, she'd have been out of a job a long time ago.

But she was independent, a contractor, a player who analyzed and determined her own comfort level of risk.

Hers was off the chart, and a whole boatload of otherwise tough guys wouldn't work with her because of it. Hawkins didn't have a problem with her. Hundreds of hours of drills and endless rounds of repetition had hardwired the girl to obey him on command. Kid had the same advantage. C. Smith worked with her, because according to him, even with her little "problems," she was far more reliable than a whole helluva lot of DEA and FBI agents he'd been teamed with—and don't even ask him about the CIA jerks he'd suffered through. It was no surprise to Smith that Royce had been recruited, trained, and employed by the Central Intelligence Agency.

Travis hated working with her, but he'd always rather it was him than anyone else. It didn't matter that she had the skills to do the job. There was a part of him that never forgot she'd been Gillian Pentycote before she'd become Red Dog, and Gillian couldn't have "smoked" a man at eight hundred meters to save her life.

Red Dog could—and did—routinely, without even having to work at it.

Hell, Gillian couldn't have done it at ten meters—and that was the third strike against her as far as he was concerned, right after her "lost" moments, and her damn arm.

Failure of will got more people killed than equipment malfunctions. Red Dog knew the price of failure and had the single-minded will to win every single time, always acting without hesitation or mercy. But Gillian would hesitate. She would think instead of act, wondering if she was doing the right thing. In one of those unpredictable split seconds of indecision, he could lose her—and nothing in the last two years had convinced him that Gillian wasn't still there, a sweet but deadly softness somewhere within the psyche of the hard woman called Red Dog.

Especially not the way she made love.

Her hand slid down between his legs, and she cupped his balls, playing with him as she sucked his tongue into her mouth.

Oh, yeah. That was definitely getting him where he wanted to go, especially when she slid her hand back up and started stroking him.

The girl had good hands, and he let her set the pace and tease him, because the longer he waited, the more of her he got. At least that had been his first thought, but with each stroke, with every time she tightened her palm around him and drove him a little closer to the edge, he remembered how long it had been since he'd been with her, and his thoughts, first and otherwise, started focusing on having something sweeter and more intense on him than her hand—and lovely girl, she was thinking the same thing. It was easy to tell.

Kiss by soft, wet kiss, she worked her way down his body, until she was on her knees and had him in her mouth, her hand still stroking him, her tongue, hot and silky, snaking over the top of him. He reached behind her and turned off the water, and it was all so perfect, the heat and steam, the utter relaxation of his mind, and Gillian—going down on him.

Sometimes the girl liked to be in charge, of everything, and he didn't mind. Oh, hell, no.

Leaning back against the shower wall, he thrust

his hips forward, his hand gently cupping the back of her head. He thrust again, and she took more of him. Again, and he went even deeper. *Geezus*.

Minute after endless minute of pleasure doubled over on each other, the rhythm of her mouth, the hot, wet glides of her tongue down the length of him and back up, and the sucking—God, he loved it. She didn't stop, just kept taking him higher, winding him up tighter with her hands and mouth, until inevitably, irresistibly, she took him to orgasm. Braced against the wall, he went rigid and just let it happen, just the way she liked it, his muscles straining, his cock so hard inside the softness of her mouth, and pure, hot pleasure pouring out of him.

She held him where he stood, until he was finished. When she released him, he bent his knees and slid down to be with her on the shower floor. Gathering her in his arms, he took her mouth in a deep kiss and slid one hand down between her legs. She was so soft to the touch, so beautiful, so wonderfully, erotically wet—and she could count on him, every time.

"Come on, sweetheart," he said, bringing her with him to her feet as he stood up. "Let's go have some fun in bed."

H ONORIA "HONEY" YORK had been warned about traveling to El Salvador. Third World slumming, her father had called it, something best left to others, though he hadn't named the "others."

He hadn't needed to. Everyone knew the name.

Not much shopping, her mother had cautioned, and therefore not much to do with one's time.

Her oldest brother, Thomas, had suggested his place on St. Barts, if she really felt the need to get away. Two of her other brothers had decided to take Thomas up on his offer and left a week ago with a few cases of Dom and a small posse of up-and-coming models. Her fourth brother was temporarily out of touch while on an expedition to the North Pole to draw attention to his latest political cause, global warming. It was working. He had a BBC crew with him, and an independent film-maker who had cut a deal with the Discovery Channel for any exclusive polar bear footage that came out of the grand adventure, and a deal with *Rolling Stone* for any footage of her brother's rock-and-roll-star girlfriend doing anything in fur and a pair of mukluks.

Grand, outrageous adventures—that's what the York family had, what they'd been having since the first York had left the family estates in England over two hundred years ago and braved their way to the New World and a whole new level of wealth and social notoriety.

Yorks did not have dangerous encounters in pestilent hotel rooms with ill-kempt men carrying guns. At least no York in good standing ever had until today, a tricky designation at best, and no one talked about the Yorks not in good standing. There was only one, actually, the one who had gotten Honoria into hot water up to her neck again. Then she'd gone and all by herself made it so much worse.

Oh, God. She should have known better than to take any advice offered by Elliot "Kip" Fletcher-Wooten III. Anyone who had graduated from Harvard and taken less than ten years to wash up in Puerto Vallarta, Mexico, as the manager of a beachside cabana resort with a high-season rack rate of less than two hundred dollars a night was obviously from the shallow end of the Fletcher-Wooten gene pool.

Actually, any male over the age of three who allowed himself to be called "Kip-Woo" had probably been doomed from the start. The same, she realized, might be said of any female over the age of three who allowed herself to be called "Honey," and God knew, she was well over the age of three—and God knew, she was having a dangerous encounter in a pestilent hotel room with an ill-kempt man carrying a gun.

Two guns, actually, his and hers.

She stifled a groan. How in the world had she let that happen? And what in the world was going to happen next?

Oh, God, she didn't want to know.

She was shaking so badly, and she could hardly catch her breath, and her heart was in her throat, which was a perfectly crappy place for it to be.

So help her God, if she got out of this alive, she was going to personally strangle Kip-Woo for hooking her up with Javier, a bellhop at the Royal Suites Hotel, who had hooked her up with Rey, a busboy at the Caribe Inn, who had hooked her up with Hector, the guy on the street who had cheated her out of two bullets. One block, that's all she'd gone, one block into no-man's-land, in a cab that had summarily deserted her at the first sign of trouble, to buy a gun to protect herself in a country where she had no business being in the first place.

It was all so ridiculously clear now, the same way it was so ridiculously clear that she should have strangled Kip years ago, when his neck had still been small enough for her to get her hands around, before he'd grown up and become her co-conspirator, confidant, and all-around *idiot* best friend with connections to unsavory people like Hector.

The nameless one deserved house arrest, but house arrest had never worked on that one before, and she doubted if it would now.

To his credit, Kip had warned her not to travel to El Salvador alone, especially to San Luis. Things had been a bit unstable in San Luis of late, he'd said; some bad elements had moved in.

No kidding. She'd seen nothing but bad elements since she'd left her lovely hotel and gotten in that damn cab, which she shouldn't have done. Hindsight was always so perfect. Any woman with an ounce of sense would have listened to Kip, or her father, or her debutante advisor from the year of her "coming out," who had also warned her not to travel to El Salvador, especially alone. Her colorist had warned her. The valet at Saks had warned her. Never travel alone, they'd said, and never, ever travel alone when going abroad, which for her colorist meant any place other than Manhattan, L.A., or Washington, D.C., and absolutely everything below the Mason-Dixon Line.

El Salvador was below the Mason-Dixon, far, far below, but technically speaking, as of one minute ago, she was no longer alone. She had a bodyguard with a gun who did not work for the State Department and whose name probably wasn't John Roland.

No wonder it was so hard to breathe.

"If you pass out, that's going to be a bad thing," her "bodyguard" said without shifting his gaze from the door.

Yes, she knew that, thank you. For one thing, it meant she'd end up on a very questionable-looking floor, because he did not look like he was going to take the time to catch her if she started sliding down the wall.

He was too damn busy watching the door and waiting, focused, and looking damned deadly with the way he was holding his gun, which oddly enough almost made her feel safe.

It shouldn't. She'd been insane to let him drag her into his room. She wasn't sure how she could have stopped him. He'd moved so fast, almost as fast as when he'd taken her gun, which still made her head spin.

She'd thought she'd had a good plan, that she'd gotten her ducks in a row by arranging to buy some protection, but oh, hell, no. Her ducks were running around in circles, in a dead panic, breathless and terrified—exactly like her, except she was glued to the wall. He'd said not to move a muscle, and she hadn't, not one since she'd plastered herself into the corner.

"Don't worry," he said, slanting her a quick glance. "If those men come through the door, you're going to get your money's worth."

Somehow, that was not a very comforting thought, that he could deliver five hundred dollars' worth of violence in five minutes or less, especially when the message was delivered in such a stone-cold tone of voice.

"D-do you know them?"

"Only by reputation."

And that didn't sound good. Oh, no, not at all.

"Wh-what kind of reputation?"

His gaze slid to her again, his face grim, and suddenly—oh, quite suddenly—all she wanted to do was run.

"Don't," he said, which disconcerted the hell out of her.

"Y-you can't possibly be reading my mind."

"I don't have to. Every thought you have is written on your face." He turned back to the door, and she heard him mutter something about "must be a goddamn awful way to live."

It was. She let out a shaky sigh, trying to buck up, think clearly, and trying very hard not to cry.

"Do *not* cry," he said very succinctly, shooting her another quick glance, his voice taking on a very cold edge.

Damn him.

"That'll bring them right down on top of us," he warned.

And oh, God, she didn't want to do that. She was so out of her element. So far out.

And she wanted back in—back into Saks and valet parking, back into cosmopolitans, one of which she could use right now, and most immediately back into the safety of her suite at the Royal.

Relative safety, she reminded herself between short, shallow breaths she was doing her damnedest to slow down and deepen. The explosion last night had been less than two blocks from her hotel. The burned-out hulks of the two cars that had been set aflame two nights ago were still smoldering in the San Luis Yacht Club's parking lot.

"Wh-what is your name? Your real name?" She really should know, just in case she survived.

He shook his head once and turned his attention back to the door, and she decided he probably could read her mind, because she'd sure as hell just read his. His name wasn't any of her business, not for love or money. Five minutes, five hundred dollars, and then she was on her own.

In El Salvador—oh, God, what was going on out there? Where were those men? The ones with the really big guns? She'd heard them come into the hotel behind her, talking, one guy shouting orders and scaring the holy crap out of her. She'd all but flown up the stairs, and practically fallen right on top of—*him*.

Her gaze dropped down the length of her "bodyguard," from top to bottom, then went back up: camouflage boots, baggy cargo pants, and the rest of him, all wrapped in a faded and worn gray T-shirt and a once-upon-a-time-blue parrot shirt—shoulders, chest, arms.

Especially shoulders.

And chest.

And arms.

He worked out.

A lot.

Messy haircut, scruffy stubble along his jaw, short nose, small mouth, high cheekbones, dark eyebrows, and Ray-Bans, aviator style. Slouched in his chair in front of the cantina, a beer bottle dangling from his fingers, he'd looked like a thousand other slackers she'd seen in dozens of other tropical beach towns all over the world.

But standing in a grade D hotel room with no air-conditioning, with his gun drawn, he looked like the Great Wall of China, like it would take more than a horde of Huns to get through him, and with that realization came another: He really was a bodyguard.

For real.

Kip-Woo had a gun. He'd even taken her shooting and shown her how to use it before she'd left Puerto Vallarta to come to San Luis. But even with a gun in his hand, and even at six feet two, Honey doubted if it would take much more than a disgruntled guest or a drunken bar patron to get through Kip.

Mr. You Don't Need to Know My Name wasn't six feet of anything, but he was built like the Rock of Gibraltar, steady and solid from the inside out, and suddenly, for no other reason than that, she knew she was going to get through the next five minutes, no matter what those minutes brought.

After that, she'd be on her own again, but as long as he was standing there, willing and able—obviously *very* able—and ready to put his life on the line for five hundred dollars, she was safer than she'd been since she'd left the family mansion in

Washington, D.C., with a quarter of a million in cold cash hidden in the lining of her Louis Vuitton luggage.

Kip knew what she'd brought with her. He was the only one who knew, and to his credit, he'd done more than warn her off El Salvador. He'd *begged* her not to go, especially smuggling contraband, and she wouldn't have, not in a quarter of a million years, except for Julia Ann-Marie York, the black sheep of the York family and the only sister she had.

CHAPTER

7

GILLIAN STOOD NAKED in the shadows behind the open set of French doors in her loft, looking out over the garage's second-floor garden. Lush greenery and the kaleidoscopic colors and sweet scents of hundreds of flowers in full bloom filled the rooftop.

The sun was sliding behind the mountains, the air cooling and blowing gently across her skin, the quiet before the storm. Sometimes, every now and then, when she least expected it, all the jumbled-up pieces of her past would streak like a bolt of lightning across her brain, frying synapses and circuits, and throwing her into an abyss of chaos.

Tonight that was not going to happen, because something else was. She felt it. There was blood on the wind.

She took a long, steady breath, letting it spiral into her body, lazy and gentle, and fill her lungs. Tonight there would be death. Here.

Before . . . before the night in the white room, she didn't think she'd known things, not the way she knew things now. XT7, the drug she'd been given, was complicated, its effect on women untested and undocumented except on her, and it had fucked her up good. Her memories had been wiped clean. Other portions of her brain were walled off. She could feel the walls, but she couldn't get around them.

And another part of her brain had been opened up, unblocked, let loose: prescience, a stream of it, not always good for anything, but sometimes good for what she needed. Like tonight.

She let her breath out, slow and easy, and softened her gaze. The El Salvador mission had been flawless. She'd been like a cat in the dark, and before she'd been a cat slipping over Royce's walls, she'd been the bad bitch Red Dog. Those poor little *mareros*, the gang-bangers, in Mara Plata had never imagined anyone like her. They'd never imagined the promise of their lousy lives getting even worse.

She wasn't a social worker. She wasn't out to save tattooed teenage boys with ink on their faces, and ink on their arms, and no prospects beyond the trinity of dots they wore like a badge on their skin: hospital, prison, and the grave. Anyone who dealt with Royce was her enemy.

Everyone who dealt with Royce was her enemy.

The Central American gangs were violent in the extreme. Those boys expected to die badly. She couldn't scare them with death—so she'd found the one gangster at the top of the San Luis heap with the pull to make a decision, and she'd given him the name of a buyer he would want to deal with more than Royce, the buyer she'd given to everyone she'd wanted to take away from the ex-CIA agent.

Fuck. She knew some bad people. She'd killed some, manipulated others, and did business with one: Sir Arthur Kendryk, Lord Weymouth. Kendryk ate gangs like Mara Plata for his noon luncheon. In the month he'd held her captive, she'd seen him do it, wipe a Third World network and power base right off the map with a sweep of his hand.

The San Luis *mara* would never know what hit them, if they screwed with Kendryk, or if they didn't meet their quotas, or if he simply decided he no longer needed them. The Lord of Weymouth did not leave loose ends—except for her.

For her, he would take the Mara Plata deal, the way he'd taken the other four deals she'd ruined for Royce. In the realities of Kendryk's world, Mara Plata barely registered on the scale, and then only if the whole, international scope of the gang was taken into consideration.

For her, he'd dealt with the Uzbek, Gul Rashid, and given him a premium price on a shipment of Afghan opium.

For her, he'd broken his golden rule—he'd felt pity, then suffered as pity had turned to empathy and the death stroke of love. Nothing about the fact made him happy. So he fought it with the arrogance of his wealth, with the power of his intellect, and with the icy coolness of his most disdainful regard.

And yet he was there, always . . . for her.

Behind her, she heard Travis rise from the bed. The angel didn't know about Kendryk. No one did, not Skeeter, not Kid, not even Superman.

But it was the angel who would be hurt the worst.

She let her eyes drift closed and took another soft breath.

She could still feel him, still feel where Travis had been inside her, could still feel the pleasure he'd given her. No one made love like the angel boy, and certainly not the devil named Kendryk.

And yet . . . and yet . . . For a moment, no longer,

she halted her breath, held it inside, then released it gently back into the night.

And yet Kendryk was a part of her, too, for better or for worse, and there wasn't a doubt in her mind that it was going to be for worse, that someday he would demand a price it would kill her to pay—and she would pay it anyway.

She took another breath and slowly opened her eyes. The shadows were deepening across the garden, melding into one darkness, the veil of night spreading out from the horizon.

Sometimes she didn't like herself very much, and the weeks she'd been with Kendryk had been the worst of those times. She didn't know for sure, couldn't know for sure, but she didn't think the woman she'd been before the XT7 would have made the choices Red Dog had made. Or maybe the will to live that beat so strongly in her heart had always been there, the bone-deep conviction that she would do anything—*anything*—to survive. Having "died" once, it was not an experience she wanted to repeat.

So she'd done what she'd had to do. She'd made her deal, sealed the pact, and reaped the unexpected rewards of having Sir Arthur Kendryk at her back.

Smoothing her hand low across her belly, she let out a sigh and waited. Travis moved quietly, but she could sense his growing nearness, sense the warmth of his desire and the warmth of his body reaching out to surround her. When she felt him come to a stop behind her, when she felt his hand slide around her waist and draw her close, another, softer sigh left her.

He was shameless, this boy who loved her. All of twenty-four years old when they'd met, he'd known more about her body than she had, known more about what she'd needed, more about what she'd wanted. To this day, he knew more about giving her pleasure than he should.

"Close your eyes," he said quietly, his mouth brushing across the back of her neck.

Yes...she let her lashes fall and inhaled the scent of a thousand flowers.

"Bow your head." His voice was so sure, so gentle, and yet so undeniably male.

She obeyed.

"Submission," he whispered with a soft laugh, and she felt his teeth graze her skin, so lightly at first, then harder, never enough to mark her, but enough to let her know he was there, in control, and that if he so chose, she would be *helpless*... *helpless*.

Poor little Gillian Pentycote, so helpless, bound and gagged. So frightened. So terrified.

The angel slipped a loop of soft rope around her

wrist and drew it tight. Then he wrapped the rope around one of the brackets he'd set into the wall above the French doors and pulled, surely, steadily, until she was stretched taut with only her toes touching the floor, her arm raised above her head.

"I'm not . . . I'm not sure I want—"

"Yes, you do," he said, his voice so calm.

And he was right.

The blindfold came next, tight enough for her to feel, tight enough for her to know it wasn't going to accidentally fall off.

There were no accidents in this game. Never.

The cloth was soft. She felt the edges of it across the bridge of her nose and across her eyebrows, creating darkness, the place of fear.

The loss of sight was complete.

Her breath started to come short, running along the edge of panic, and his mouth came down on hers in a drugging kiss. Wet, serious, taking and wanting, his tongue pushing deep, again and again, consuming her mouth, demanding more, and she gave him everything she had. It was the only way. She slid her free hand up into his hair, tangling her fingers through the long strands, holding him close and moving her mouth with his, pressing herself against him, curves molding to angles, the firm softness of her body coming up against the rock hardness of his. The taste of him filled her, the gentleness of his breath against her skin, the strength of his arms around her.

Then he was gone, and she felt a strip of soft cloth going around and around the bottom half of her face, covering her mouth, fitting snugly against her jaw, wrapping around the back of her head and coming up the other side, binding her, stealing her voice, enough cloth to keep her from being able to scream.

Her heart started to beat faster, to race, and his hand was there, sliding up her torso and cupping her left breast, his palm warm, his fingers callused but gentle.

Her panic eased, but an edge of fear remained and grew sharper when his hand left her and she felt him at her feet, tying her ankles together with the other end of the rope. It took some time, the intricacy of the knots and stringing the rope through the ring in the floor, to keep her from being able to move, at all, in any direction.

When he was finished at her feet, he brought the same rope up and tied it around her waist. The tug of each successive knot tightened the one before, one after the other. She knew what came after her waist, and she started to fight, but he caught her to him hard, his hand capturing her free arm and holding it behind her back.

He tied it there, tied her wrist to the rope at her

back, and she was in bondage, in the limbo of the unknown. Fear and anticipation rolled through her, holding her in place more surely than the ropes, bringing her to a perfect standstill, balanced on her toes, her raised hand gripping the rope leading from her wrist to the bracket on the wall—and being careful to breathe, she waited.

TRAVIS took a step away from her and dragged his hand back through his hair.

Geezus. What a piece of work. Just looking at her was enough to make him hard again. The arch of her feet, the length of her legs, the incredible curve of her ass, her whole body licked with a sliver of light. She damn near shimmered, her skin was so pale. Full, lush breasts, wild hair, and two bands of black across her face—it was always like this between them, dark and sweet, so hot he ached even when he was inside her, and just a little twisted.

Yeah, he needed a shrink, to love this the way he did, to love her the way he did.

Yeah, Doc, I've got this girlfriend, you see, older woman, complicated, amnesiac, and so fucking beautiful—especially when I tie her up naked in the moonlight.

Yeah, Doc, you heard it right.

And he meant tied. She wasn't going anywhere until he released her. That was the point. No half measures would do for Red Dog. The girl worked without a net—all the time, every time.

And every time, she pushed him straight to the edge. The gag and the blindfold kept him right there, balanced on the edge between his commitment and his conscience. It was a damned uncomfortable place to be—and yet it turned him on. Someday, he was going to look into that, kind of check himself out, see what the fuck was up with him; until then, he just went with it—to a point. He'd spent days designing the rigging, testing the knots, practicing tying them. Timing was everything with this gig, and when it was time to let her go, it was time to let her go. The knots needed to fall apart, and they did, every time.

But until then, she was bound.

Until then, she was his to do with as he wanted, and what he wanted was to start at the base of her throat and work his way down, all the way down, and halfway back up. That's where she wanted him, and that's where he wanted to be, at the soft, hot center of her with his tongue. She was so sleek, her body sculpted by lengths of hard muscle and the strength of the heart that kept her alive time and time again, and he loved her.

He loved her with every breath he took, and a

lot of what he loved was the mystery of her. Thirty-three years of secrets had been lost the night Souk had hit her up, but Travis didn't think thirty-three years of Gillian Pentycote's secrets came anywhere close to two years of Red Dog's.

He'd lost her once, for a month, and it had damn near driven him crazy, absofuckinglutely insane the way nothing ever had before or since. Those feelings weren't ones he was ever going to forget. Thirty days without a word, coming off the tail end of a European job that had gone bad. The kill had been made, the mission accomplished, but it had been a mess—an incapacitating but non-lethal shot, where the guy had hung on for two days in an Amsterdam hospital before dying. And there had been collateral damage, of all the damn things, a bonus in General Grant's book, one more terrorist asshole he didn't have to worry about, but the general and the rest of SDF had wondered what in the hell had happened.

She'd never said.

Never said what had happened on the hit. Never said what had happened during the god-damn month that she'd been gone.

But Travis knew.

He knew it in his heart.

Fuck.

He opened his mouth on her throat, grazing her

with his teeth and licking her skin. There were reasons he'd been so good at being the dark angel for
Nikki Chronopolous, a lot of reasons, and the bad
girl Red Dog brought all those dark reasons to
light, every one. He never hurt her, had never left a
mark on her. The ropes were tight, but not brutal.
He saved that for the job. She was stretched out
and strung up, sure, but in a minute, he'd be kneeling at her feet, and once he released the slack he'd
built into the rope at the floor ring, he would come
up between her legs and she'd be sitting on his
shoulders with his face between her thighs. It was a
sweet trip to that point, and he enjoyed every inch
of it.

But it was when he was there, with his tongue
sliding into her soft folds, and his fingers pushing
up inside her, with her tightening around him and
her body arching against him, that the last of his
tension began to lift.

Red Dog was his.

He always made it good for her in bed, but this
was where he laid his true claim, when she gave it
up for him in the lost darkness of her mind, poised
on the promise of pain, but finding pleasure instead. No one could take this journey with her to
the strange edges of her psyche better than him.
He pushed her boundaries, and then pushed far-

ther until the abyss opened up and swallowed her whole—but he never let her fall alone.

Never.

Her muffled groan sounded above him and a shudder went through her, the tremor of it running the length of her body.

Oh, yeah. He opened his mouth wider and slid his tongue over her, again and again. He knew. He knew her every reaction went straight to his groin and made him hot, made him feel heavy. He knew she tasted like heaven and an ocean of pleasure, and he knew how to get exactly what he wanted.

He slipped another finger inside her, stretching her, sliding smoothly in and out and putting pressure where she needed it the most. There was a place deep inside her imagination, a place where sexual fantasy and fact melted into one, and the path to it began here, inside the silken softness of her vagina. It wasn't enough to make her come. He'd done that for her in bed. What he needed now, what she needed, was for him to make her come apart . . . completely, totally apart.

He reached for the rope at her back with his free hand, taking hold of it just below her waist, and he pulled, stretching her tighter—and he teased her with his tongue, teased her until her groans became a sob, a soft sound of distress and longing.

Ah, Gillian . . . so sweet.

So sweet and starting to come undone for him.

He felt her first contraction, and gave the rope a short tug, freeing the hand he'd tied at her back. She immediately brought it around to the back of his head, tunneling her fingers through his hair and holding him closer, pressing herself closer, begging him to do what he was doing, only faster, only harder, and to please, please, please . . . *suck on me.*

He heard her in every cell, heard her in the back of his mind and on the tip of his tongue, and when he did it, it was all over for the bad girl. Her body went tight, her head went back, and release flooded through her, making her skin hot. He let her ride her wave of pleasure to the end, let it break over him and drive him goddamn crazy.

Fuck. He wasn't in control of this.

He wasn't in control of any goddamn thing with her, and that kept him hooked, heart and soul.

He pulled the rope and felt it loosen, felt it slip and slide and pool onto the floor, felt her do the same, her body suddenly going limp. He didn't let her fall. He never let her fall.

Never fucking ever.

He held her, keeping her close. When she was in his arms, he pulled the gag down, and with the taste of her still warm in his mouth, he kissed her, long and deep and slow, letting her taste herself, letting her know she was his . . . *only and always his.*

CHAPTER

8

SOONER OR LATER, something had to give, and C. Smith Rydell hoped to hell it was the bad guys' attention span before it was the cupcake's knees. He didn't know how in the hell somebody could shake that badly for as long as she'd kept it up and still be standing, especially on those little white platform heels.

He let his gaze run over her again where she was plastered into the corner. Cupcake was right, double frosted with sprinkles. That had to be a tough way to live, so freaking helpless, with one damn .45 cartridge to your name and not even being able to hold on to that. If she'd been his—and she wasn't—he'd teach her how to protect herself. The task would be at the top of his damn "Things

to Do Today" list—teach Cupcake how to use a
handgun. It was the only hope someone like her
had in the big bad world.

Geezus. He stepped back over to the door.
Something had to give, all right—and it sure as hell
wasn't going to be him, not an inch.

Pressing his ear to the wood panel, he listened.
Royce's men were still out there on the veranda,
deciding what to do next, then silence, quickly followed by a hurried scuffling of feet.

Party time.

He moved back away from the door and the
sudden, heavy pounding on the other side.

"Abra la puerta! Hazlo ya!" someone challenged—
Open the door. Now.

"Mierda!" Bullshit, he yelled, giving his best impression of a surly Latin drunk, which, under the
circumstances, wasn't too damn hard. *"No me mo-
leste!" Don't bother me.*

*"Buscamos a la rubia...la gringa! Abra!" We're
looking for the blonde...the American. Open up.*

Open up a solid two inches of jungle hardwood
set in a wrought-iron frame lag-bolted into the
Palacio's eight-inch-thick masonry walls and secured with two steel dead bolts?

Smith didn't think so.

He took two steps back along the wall and leveled his Sig at the unhinged side of the door frame.

"*Oígame, pendejo!*" he said, coarsening his voice and slurring his words. *Listen, asshole.* "*Si estuviese una rubia aquí, yo le cogería, no hablaría contigo! Ve te!*" *If I had a blonde in here, I'd be screwing her, not talking to you. Go away.*

Well, that shut them up, the sheer unvarnished common sense of it. But not for long.

He put his ear to the door when he heard their conversation start back up, and he had to admit that they had a pretty good plan—posting a man in the courtyard where he could observe the whole veranda, and sending two guys to the other side of the building, where they could access the balconies.

Like the balcony to his room.

Smith looked behind him at the open set of ceiling-to-floor-length windows he'd been sitting behind all day with his spotting scope. Yeah, it wouldn't take much to get through those babies, but anybody who tried was going to wish they hadn't. He could guarantee it.

"Get into the bathroom," he ordered the woman. "Into the bathtub." If all hell broke loose, the cast-iron tub was the best place for her, right after every other goddamn place in the world.

What in the hell, he wondered, was she doing in fucking El Salvador?

For that matter, what in the hell was he doing in

fucking El Salvador, except preparing to get his ass
kicked?

Gunfights, especially gunfights with four-to-one
odds, were damned tricky things.

But not as tricky as explosives.

A deafening blast from the street suddenly
rocked the room and lit up the night with a bright
flash, shattering glass and shaking the plaster off
the walls, and all-around ringing his chimes.

Geezus. Fuck.

He instinctively turned in on himself, bringing
his hands up to protect his head, too late, of course,
if the bomb had been close enough to blow him to
smithereens.

It hadn't been, and in the seconds it took him to
realize that he was still in one piece, that the hotel
hadn't collapsed, and even that there had been a
bomb, the woman disappeared.

Oh, hell, yeah. Right off the map. Poof. The
cupcake—gone.

He'd never heard of anyone being atomized by
the concussion of an explosive device, but there
wasn't anything left of her, anywhere in the room,
and the jungle hardwood door hadn't budged.

And yes, he was really starting to like that door.

But the woman, hell—he raked the room with
his gaze, and that's when he spotted a swirl of
tawny blond hair not quite held together anymore

by a red polka-dot bow peeking above the rim of the tub in the bathroom.

Okay. That was skill, pure, mad skill, to be able to move and think when glass was breaking, and the walls were shaking, and your ears had to be ringing.

Mad skill.

On the other hand, anyone who looked like her had probably realized from a pretty young age that they were going to need to be fast on their feet.

Still, he was damned impressed.

"Vamos al cuartel! Rápido!" The orders came from out on the veranda. *Back to the compound. Quickly.*

Yeah, assholes, back to the compound, he thought, and he needed to get the woman back to her hotel.

"The woman." Right. The woman probably had a name, and he definitely needed to ask her what it was. First, though, he crossed over to the broken windows, his boots crunching across shards of glass, and checked the street.

There were no body pieces anywhere, and he was damned glad of it, but the old Ford pickup that had been parked near Royce's front gate had been reduced to a burning hunk of raw scrap metal. Pieces of it were everywhere. The tires were smoldering, the upholstery was on fire, and the gate had been demolished. The two halves of wrought iron were still there, but were twisted on their hinges.

Shit. Dozens of men were racing around inside Royce's compound, more than he'd thought were in residence, and they were definitely riled up and probably going to stay that way for the rest of the friggin' night.

Dammit. He'd come to San Luis looking for Red Dog, been tagged by his old buddies in the DEA to do some recon on Royce, ended up in the middle of some half-assed Central American turf war, and had a blonde in his bathtub—a tawny-haired blonde in a low-cut dress that fit like a coat of paint.

He didn't know if it was dumb luck, or if he was just living right, or if he was fucked.

"What's your name?" he asked, a little too loudly, because he could hardly hear himself think.

A pair of large designer sunglasses peeked up over the edge of the tub.

"Honoria," she said breathlessly, and he could just imagine how fast her heart was beating. His sure as hell hadn't slowed down yet. "Honoria York, but most people call me Honey."

Yeah, he just bet they did, and for a couple hundred bucks an hour, he could probably call her Honey, too.

"Take off your glasses," he ordered. He didn't

know where in the hell that had come from particularly, but when bombs were exploding, and cars were burning, and guns were being drawn, giving orders was what he did best.

Besides, he wanted to see what she looked like from the neck up, and the glasses covered half her face. Her hair was a mess. All those little bows had given up, and so had her bobby pins. They were sticking out of her French twist here and there, and every place where a pin had fallen out, there was a curl. She had definitely lost the sleek Riviera look and was heading toward the wild side.

She reached up to take off the glasses, but whether it was because he'd told her to, or because it had gotten dark outside and was definitely dim in the room, was actually a moot point.

It didn't matter.

Not at all.

Because once the glasses came off, and he saw her face, he had the answer to his question. It wasn't dumb luck or clean living that had put her in his bathtub. It was one of those cosmic laws of the universe that had kicked in and said, "Let's screw with Rydell's head tonight, just for the hell of it."

Because she had a face guaranteed to bust him, a real heartbreaker, one of those little, goddamn pixie faces that had been his downfall more times than he cared to remember.

Honey—yeah, he just bet.

"Stay put." Another order, perfect, but it was for her own good—and his. Half a room away with a slab of cast iron between them was about as close as he wanted to get to her.

It was about as close as he dared, and that pissed him off in a way that having to face four gunmen had not. Because, *dammit*, his odds had been better against the damn gunmen. He was a helluva shot, and nothing but a sucker for a green-eyed blonde.

CHAPTER

9

GILLIAN HAD PUT the boy to bed, drugged with sex and all but knocked out. Jet lag from Thailand hadn't hurt the cause, and was probably what had actually pushed Travis over the edge into such a deep sleep. Either way, she was afraid he wasn't going to get to rest for long. His phone was going to ring in about twenty minutes, and after he took the call she'd programmed to his number, he was going to be busy the rest of the night—busy someplace else.

And she would be on her own, which was the way things had to be.

She crossed the loft again, heading toward her gun safe and letting her gaze slide over him where he lay naked on top of the sheets. He was so beautiful, his face almost sweet in sleep, like the angel he was, but there was nothing sweet about his body. Six feet of raw power and testosterone roped with muscle and sinew, he was a force to be reckoned with, a force of destruction when he so chose—and a force of near unbearable pleasure when she chose.

She let her gaze run back over the length of him and hardened herself against the easy way, against her own weakness. She had a job to do, and he couldn't be any part of it, not if she was to live with herself afterward.

And she *would* live with herself. She always did, no matter what she'd done—and she'd done things in the last two years that other people, so-called normal people, couldn't even imagine, let alone carry out.

They didn't need to, because guys like Travis, and Creed, and Hawkins were there, doing it for them. Guys like Kid and Quinn were there, watching their backs. Guys like Rydell were there, working in Central America against odds he knew he would never beat.

She was there.

And Dylan Hart was there.

She slowly came to a stop, only partway to her destination.

Dylan Hart—now, there was a name to give a girl pause, to make her think.

Hart. Yeah, definitely a name to get a girl's attention, and maybe make her break out in a sweat, a cold sweat, because that's what Hart was: cold.

Hart knew about the white room. He'd been in an identical place on the island of Sumba, Indonesia, on the receiving end of one of Dr. Souk's psychopharmaceutical concoctions, a drug known as NG4, but the NG4 hadn't changed him the way XT7 had changed her. Hart had been a ruthless son of a bitch before he'd been messed with, and he was still ruthless, still cold, still hard. He only had one soft spot in his life, and it wasn't her. Not by a long shot.

The only reason Grant let her operate through SDF was because Dylan Hart had taken personal responsibility for her, and Hart had made it very clear where the lines on his responsibility lay, and he'd made it absofuckinglutely crystal clear where her responsibilities lay.

She glanced down at the ring of keys in her hand.

She was getting ready to cross one of Hart's lines, and there were going to be repercussions. Big ones. Maybe deadly.

Her gaze went back to Travis. She loved him too much to drag him down with her into this, to have him hunted by Hart, and Hawkins, and Creed, to have General Grant sic Kid Chaos on him, to ever put him in danger of being in Kid's sights.

It could happen.

Depending on how successful she was in her quest, it *would* happen. She knew it. Hart hadn't candy-coated the facts of her employment or of her termination, and SDF would not tolerate a rogue operator. The chop-shop boys broke a lot of rules, most of the rules, but the few they kept, they held dear. Their survival depended on it, and vigilantism had no place in their operating procedures or in their hearts. They were the good guys, and not a one of them doubted it, because not a one of them had ever killed outside the law. They'd all rattled the chain of command, but none of them had ever broken it. They acted under orders, and only under orders.

She knew all this. She'd watched SDF in action. She'd read all the files. She knew the inviolate rules.

And yet...and yet... she closed her hand around the keys, so tightly she could feel the sharp edges pressing into her skin, but not so tightly that they cut. She needed her hands tonight, to hold her guns, to hold her knives, the tools of her trade. The line had already been crossed. She'd crossed it when she'd tagged Royce's walls with *Red Dog 303*, and there was no turning back.

None. Not when everything inside her pushed her on. Not when she'd been forced to her knees more times than she could bear by the monster in her mind.

If Hart wanted her after the deed was done, he was going to have to find her, and she wasn't going to let that happen. Once she started running, no one would ever find her—no one, not even the angel, and he would look.

Oh, God, he would look, except in the one place he wouldn't want to find her.

Shifting her attention back to the keys, she slipped them around on the ring. There was no other way. When she found the set she needed, she started forward again. The door on her safe was made of heavy steel, and after releasing the locks, she swung it open to reveal enough weapons and ordnance to pull off a small island coup.

Her gaze instinctively went to her sniper rifle first. The Knight SR-25 semiauto was the most powerful and longest-ranged weapon she owned, but it wasn't appropriate for the battle she saw shaping in her mind, the same battle she always saw, the one she'd war-gamed half a dozen times on the surrounding rooftops and in the alleys and the creek bed where she and Johnny Ramos, one of SDF's mechanics, paintballed.

The ACOG-scoped M4 carbine wasn't going anywhere tonight either. She'd be facing a superior force in both numbers and firepower, and she couldn't afford to get in a protracted firefight, where she could get "fixed" in position by opposing fire, flanked, and overrun. It was going to be "shoot and scoot" all night long, until she took a prisoner.

Then things were going to get serious.

Royce wouldn't come himself. He'd send his men to capture her if they could, and kill her if they had to, and one of those men was going to tell her where Royce was waiting. The ex-CIA agent truly was a sick bastard, with a misogynistic rap sheet a mile long, and she knew his first choice would be to have a little fun with the woman who'd screwed five of his deals.

Fine with her. He could want whatever his heart desired. All she needed was his location . . . all she needed was to be right tonight.

She hated to doubt herself, tried to shake it off, but prescience was a tricky thing. She'd geared up twice before, thinking Royce had found her, that the bastard had finally figured out who and what Red Dog was and was coming for her.

She'd been wrong both times.

But not tonight, she thought. Tonight felt different. Tonight she was afraid.

Reaching up, she pulled a tan, innocuous-looking briefcase off the top shelf. In a world of functional but ugly combat weapons, the pistol in the case stood apart. Perfectly balanced, finely finished, and as exquisitely crafted as a century-old Japanese *katana* blade, the TC Contender was a work of art.

She set the case on her workbench, turned the cipher lock to its combination, and popped open the top. Two scoped barrel assemblies occupied half the case, a .44 Remington Magnum threaded for a sound suppressor, and a fourteen-inch .223 Remington, both set into custom-formed green felt recesses. The frame and forestock of the pistol occupied the lower right corner of the case, with the remaining recesses filled with cleaning supplies and a hand-tooled leather cartridge cuff she wore cinched around her right forearm for fast reloads.

She gently ran her fingers over the polished ebony grip and traced the silver-inlaid dragon scrollwork etched into the frame. The Contender was pure Buck Rogers, black and beautiful, blued steel with a long sensual curve on the trigger guard, its grip custom-raked to fit her hand. And its purpose—its only real purpose—was to kill things; more specifically, in her line of work, to kill people.

Like Anthony F. Royce.

The weapon's only disadvantage was its break-open, single-shot action—only one round could be loaded and fired at a time. But Gillian could fire, load, and fire again in less than six seconds, and she could do it with dead-on accuracy, hitting a silhouette's center chest ring ten out of ten times at 150 meters with her .223 barrel and a 69-grain match bullet loaded to 2,820 feet per second.

Kid had trained her well, and so had Superman. With the Contender for offense, and her Trijicon .40 caliber long-slide Glock for defense, she had the lightest, most compact package possible for the night ahead.

All she needed was for her enemy to come to Denver, for Royce to finally come after her.

FROM THE DEPTHS of a cast-iron tub that had seen better days, Honey searched through her tote bag. She needed a smoke. Honest to God, and if she couldn't find one of those little cigarillos she'd dropped in there this afternoon, she just might—

Oh, hell, she didn't know what she'd do. Do without, that was for damn sure, but other than that, her options were damn slim.

Dress casual, Julia had said. *Bring the money to the church, St. Mary's. Father Bartolo will be there at eight o'clock.*

Honey checked her watch and swore under her breath. She was going to be late, as usual. But my God, a bomb had just gone off in the street.

Her hands were still shaking. She wasn't sure,

but she thought her heart was shaking, too, inside her chest. Her ears hurt. Her shin hurt where she'd hit it diving into the bathtub, and her butt hurt for no reason other than she was sitting in a bathtub with no water, no bubbles, no scented oils, no—

Oh, thank God. She'd found a cigarillo.

More rummaging produced a book of matches. That had been good thinking, she told herself, to grab the matches off the reception desk this afternoon before she'd left the Royal Suites Hotel to begin her big awful adventure. Much more good thinking like that and she'd probably end up dead.

She stuck the cigarillo between her lips, struck a match, then held the trembling flame to the small cigar. A couple of puffs later, she was in business: smoking, in a rusty bathtub, with plaster falling off the walls and landing on her dress.

Gripping the cigarillo between her teeth, she brushed at the bits and flakes of gold-painted plaster. The whole situation was tawdry in the extreme, and to think she could have been on St. Bart's with maid service and a live-in cook—and no bombs.

Julia Ann-Marie needed her bottom paddled, but Honey didn't think the church allowed anyone to paddle a nun's bottom.

A nun. Good God, the York family was still

reeling: a papist in their midst, and even more amazing, a woman sworn to virginity.

Honey inhaled, choked a bit, got it all back under control, and started looking for one of those little bottles of booze she'd snagged off the plane this morning.

She needed her gun back, and Mr. You Don't Need to Know My Name could either give it to her or give her two hundred dollars—but she wanted the gun. It wasn't safe to be in San Luis without a gun, certainly not where she was going. Anything could happen on her way to the bakery, and she needed to be prepared with something besides a book of matches, a small cigar, and a shot of bourbon under her belt.

Though, truth be told, things could be worse. Things could always be worse, but they weren't, so she wasn't going to think about it.

Her next breath was a little ragged on the end, and she started searching harder for the bourbon. She remembered "worse." She would never forget "worse," no matter how long she lived, so what in the hell was she doing in Central America again? Anywhere in Central America?

Saving Sister Julia's orphans, was the answer. Good little WASP that she was, she'd taken on a painfully compelling mission of mercy for the Catholic Church, and all she needed was a smoke and a bottle of bourbon, or vodka, or gin, or whatever came up first, to steady her nerves.

Oh, hell, yes, Honey York knew exactly what she was doing, which was not freaking out in a bathtub.

Maybe a Xanax was in order.

Sure it was, and the bottle of tiny white pills had to be in her damn tote bag somewhere, probably rolling around with the booze, which she finally found. Her hand had barely closed around a bottle, though, when the lights went out.

"Fuck." That came straight out of Mr. You Don't Need to Know My Name's mouth, and she couldn't have agreed more.

She heard him crunching across the broken glass on the far side of the room. When the beam of his flashlight hit her full in the face, it darn near blinded her.

"Are you okay?" he asked.

"No." She instinctively lifted her hand in front of her eyes.

"You're drinking." It was a flat statement, not a question, and she wasn't sure, but she thought she detected just the slightest amount of censure in his voice. "And smoking."

"Yes." She was having a drink, and a smoke, or at least trying to have a drink, and if he didn't like it, he could suck eggs.

Then the lights came back on—thank God.

She checked the bottle in her hand. She'd gotten one of the gin bottles, which really wasn't a good idea. She always got a little excitable on gin. It was a family trait. She dropped it back in her tote and rustled around some more.

"Great. Lights," he said. "That's better."

It would be, if she could find the bourbon.

"Come on out of there, Ms. York," he continued, putting his flashlight back in one of the cargo pockets on his pants, "and I'll get you back to your hotel."

"No."

"No?"

Aha—bourbon. She lifted the small bottle out of her tote and twisted off the lid, but before she could get it to her mouth, another explosion rocked the room, a big one, from farther up the street, and all the lights went out again.

"Fuck."

Exactly, and then some. She was frozen in the tub, every cell in her body trembling. All the air in the room had just pushed in on her, hard, like a shove, then released. Big chunks of plaster were falling off the walls. She could feel them landing on her, and she'd actually bounced. Just a little, but enough to scare her spitless. She could die here, for the love of God.

One lousy day in San Luis, one lousy plane hop from her beach cabana in Puerto Vallarta, and she could die.

She'd have to skip the Xanax, goddammit. Dying *calmly* was completely out of the question.

He flipped his flashlight back on and beamed it in her face, the jerk. "What hotel are you staying at, Ms. York? I'm not going to ask again."

Good.

"I—I want my g-gun back, and my bullet."

That got her a dose of stone-cold silence.

"I'll return them to you when you're back at your hotel," he finally said.

"I-I'm not going back to my hotel." She pressed the bottle to her lips and tilted it back.

Oh, God, that felt good, a warm stream of bourbon running down her throat.

"Why not?"

She choked once, then caught her breath and let out a little cough. "I'm—I'm on a mission of mercy." Not that it was any of his business.

Whatever he said to that, and he said quite a bit, he said it in Spanish, which was just as well. She didn't need his opinion, or his approval, and she did not need a translation. His tone had said it all, and quite frankly, she was offended.

He turned and headed back into the bedroom. She heard him crunching around on the broken glass, prowling while he went through his sotto voce tirade. When a small flame flared up in the bedroom, she realized he'd been looking for a candle.

Then he was back, looming over her and anchoring the candle on an iron shelf bolted into the wall behind the bathtub.

"Mission of mercy," he said, straightening up, his voice so cold, he could have owned the patent. "Explain what you mean by a mission of mercy."

Screw him.

"I owe you five hundred dollars, not an explanation," she said in a voice that, despite the tremor in it, she thought was cool enough to put him in his place.

She was wrong.

"THE price for my services just went up, then. You want to stay in my bathtub? Great. It's going to cost you two grand to get out."

Mission of mercy, his ass. Smith wasn't buying it for a split second. In that dress, the only mercy she was dishing out was to that rich old guy who'd lost her, and that guy was going to be looking for her, looking hard, him and whoever else he could pull in on the search, beginning with the police. Smith bet a dozen people had seen her run into the

Palacio, and he'd be damned if he let her be found in his room.

Like it or not, she was going back where she'd come from.

"B-but that's—that's . . ." She looked up at him, words failing her.

Just as well. He wasn't in the mood to hear any dissent.

"And every minute you stay in my bathtub is going to cost you another thousand dollars." This could be his best "get rich quick" scheme yet. Not that he'd had many.

"I am *not* paying to stay in your bathtub."

Perfect.

"Then you better start setting up house, sweetheart, because you ain't getting out."

"The hell I'm not." She clamped her cigarillo between her teeth and started to struggle to her feet, a pretty good trick in platform heels inside a cast-iron tub. "You . . . you can't make me—"

"Oh, yes, I can." He reached for her, his hand closing on her waist, the other grabbing for her tote before the whole kit and caboodle of her toppled back into the tub.

What in the hell, he thought, hefting the tote in his hand. It weighed a ton.

Still holding her around the waist, he lifted the

bag away from her, and wondered why he hadn't just thought of that in the first place.

"You . . . you—" She made a grab for it, but it was no contest. He just held it higher.

"Yeah, yeah, me." Her hotel key was bound to be in the bag, along with all her identification and anything else he might like to know, and he should have figured all that out about two minutes ago. The only possible excuse he'd accept was the car bomb and whatever else had been blown to smithereens out on the street. Explosives had a way of riveting a guy's attention.

"You can't." She made another small lunge for the tote, and rather than let her fall on her face, he used her forward momentum to help swing her over the side of the tub—and he checked his watch.

"You owe me three thousand dollars." He knew women, and this one was small, a hundred and ten, a hundred and fifteen pounds max—and just about ready to come out of that dress. The whole polka-dotted wonder of it had gotten a bit twisted around in the tub, and her jacket had slipped off one shoulder.

Geezus.

"You can go to hell." She pulled the jacket back up, for all the damn good that did. It was teeny, and covered up exactly nothing.

"Been there, done that."

"Oh, for crying out loud," she said, taking the cigarillo out from between her teeth and exhaling a cloud of smoke. "You can't try to rescue me one second and steal my bag the next. It doesn't make sense."

"The only thing that doesn't make sense is you, in San Luis, on the wrong side of town, in that dress."

"There is nothing wrong with my dress," she said, using both her hands to pull the dress down and smooth it into place—adjusting the halter top, kind of shaking herself back into it, a move that all but froze him to the floor. "It's off the rack, that's all. I was *told* to dress casual."

Finishing up, she slid her palms over her hips and tugged at the hem.

Off the rack. Right. *Casual.*

"Who told you to dress casual?"

"None of your business." She finished her adjustments, looked up at him, and took a long drag off the cigarillo. "Give me back my bag."

Her hands were trembling, the cigar was trembling, and she was standing there in a pair of bow-tied platform heels, not even close to reaching his shoulder height, trying to hold her own against him.

She couldn't do it. Not on a bet. Not on any day of the week.

"No." Hell, she couldn't even hold her own against her hairdo. The curls had won, big time, a riot of them. They were all topsy-turvy, going every which way, with the polka-dot bows stuck here and there, looking ridiculous.

But she didn't look ridiculous. No way. She looked tumbled.

Right.

He let out his breath. Whoever had lost her should be shot. She was pure hothouse, and tonight, San Luis was jungle all the way.

Lucky for her, he was a jungle boy—and he was going to get her back to her hotel. All he needed was her key or a receipt with the hotel's name.

With that in mind, he headed into the bedroom, planning on upending the tote onto the bed and finding what he needed.

She was right on his heels.

"I mean it, Mr. . . . Mr.—"

"Smith."

"Mr. Smith? Oh, right." She didn't sound like she believed him for a minute. "I want my bag, now."

She tried to flank him and make a grab for it, to no avail, of course. He just held it higher.

"Smith is my first name," he corrected her, then stopped for a second as another explosion rocked the night. *Dammit*. It wasn't as close as the first two, sounding like it was coming from over by the marina, but it was still another goddamn explosion. "Actually, it's my middle name, so there's no Mr. anything here. Just Smith."

Fuck. He couldn't do it. He could dump her bag, was planning on it, but he couldn't dump her. Not with the whole goddamn town coming apart from the beach to the barrio. No matter where she was staying on tourist row, the building would be cheap, hollow cinder-block construction. Not damn much protection. A 7.62 round would go right through the walls—a fact he knew from personal, tactical experience, and yes, he'd gotten his guy. A car bomb on the street would take the walls clean out.

But the Palacio, the damned decrepit Palacio was solid. Hardwood doors, hardwood floors, and those eight-inch-thick masonry walls.

So hell, no. He wouldn't be taking her back tonight. He was stuck with her. Stuck with her dumb polka-dot bows, stuck with her damn dress—he turned the tote bag upside down and let everything fall out on the bed—stuck with a couple hundred thousand dollars in U.S. currency rubber-banded in two-inch-thick bundles of fifty-dollar bills.

Fuck. And he really meant it this time.

CHAPTER

WOMEN AND GUNS were a deadly sexy combination, Travis thought, especially when the woman was Gillian and she was putting together her custom TC Contender—naked.

With anyone else the question would have been why was she putting it together at all? Not so with Red Dog. Stay ready, be prepared, those were her watchwords, the mantra that kept her head in the right place.

He stretched in the bed, then propped himself up with a few of her zillion pillows, settling in to watch her work. He didn't put too much effort into getting comfortable, but it didn't take much to catch Red Dog's attention. She had a raptor's instincts to respond to even the slightest movement.

She slanted him a long look from where she was working at her loading bench.

"Hey," she said. "Are you rested?"

"Almost." He grinned. There was no way to get enough rest on their first night together in a month. Or on their second. Or on their third. By the end of the week, when they were finally getting used to being back together, without fail, one of them or both of them would get called back out.

He honestly didn't think about her too much when he was on a mission, except when the mission concerned her, like his and Kid's trip to Thailand, where they'd been tracking Tony Royce. For the kind of work he usually did for Steele Street, the work he did with Creed Rivera, thinking about anything except the job at hand was not an option.

Running through South American jungles with Creed had taken everything he'd had in the beginning, and sometimes more than he'd had. He'd been in the best shape of his life and a good nine years younger than Rivera, and he'd still had to bust his ass to keep up.

"Superior genetics, *pendejo*," Creed had told him with a shit-eating grin one time when Travis had been doubled over, puking his guts out on some jungle trail, and Creed had barely been breathing hard.

Travis didn't think two years on the team had changed his genetics much, but it had changed everything else. When someone's life depended on how fast they could move with all the gear they might need to do a job better than anybody else in the world, or at least better than anybody who might be looking for them, the words "being in shape" took on a whole new meaning.

His gaze went over Gillian where she'd turned back to her workbench and the Contender. She was drop-dead gorgeous, and there wasn't a man who saw her who didn't respond to that beauty, to her wild-girl looks. She was strong and sleek, her body perfectly formed, her hair a deep, rich shade of auburn that for seventy-five bucks every six weeks, a stylist over on Larimer Street kept looking like she'd just stepped out of a wind tunnel.

She was tough, as tough as Superman when she had to be, and she never stopped when she had to keep going. She was "good in the woods" whether the woods were tropical, temperate, flat-out desert, or urban, and she could keep up with Creed without breaking a sweat. Travis had seen her do it.

But he never forgot the way she'd been the first night they'd met, the night he'd first made love with her. She'd been sweet, and sweetly scatter-brained that night, not tough. She'd been soft and so incredibly female, so incredibly giving to fall into his arms and lap and everything else and just give herself up to him.

To remember that and to see the way she was now was hard. The changes in her had been wrought by more than training and dedication, by more than her will. The drug she'd been given had had a decisive and undeniable hand in what she had become. XT7 had hardened her body, made her lean. She only kept her weight up by working at it. The parameters impressed upon her mind and psyche and soul by the drug had changed her face. Her features were the same, but her expressions were different, because the muscles now responded differently to emotional stimuli, and a lot of the time, they didn't respond much. Her eyes were still a warm, amber brown, but he'd seen them glint almost yellow with a cold fierceness that had frozen more than one man in his tracks.

It wasn't guilt that held him to her side, though he'd never forgiven himself for letting her go up alone to the room in the Hotel Lafayette the night she'd been abducted. He should have been with her. He'd been armed, he'd been trained, and she'd had neither of those advantages.

She'd been helpless.

She'd been tortured.

And nothing had been the same for her since.

So he tied her up sometimes, when she wanted

sex that way, and he thought about it a lot, and he worried about it a little. Bondage had never been part of his sex life or his sexual imprinting techniques before, but he'd studied it, studied the psychology of it, and yeah, he figured the two of them were right on track—just a little fucked up.

Hell.

"Tell me about Panama."

She'd said it had been rough.

"Rydell did the recon, and it was good," she said, lifting the .223 barrel with its attached scope out of the tan case. "So when I got there, he had things pretty well set up, including how we were going to work with the local authorities." With the frame, forestock, and barrel ready, she began assembling the Contender for its long-range capacity. It took just under a minute, and when she was done, she opened the action and looked through the barrel.

He knew what she'd see: nothing. She never left a speck of fouling in her barrels.

"Hawkins said you were looking for car bombs." SDF had been called in by special request to neutralize five Colombian cartel terrorists who reportedly had two car bombs hidden somewhere in Panama City and were planning on using those bombs to attack either an American facility or one of the Panamanian government offices.

"The local boys were looking for the bombs,"

she said. "Rydell and I were looking for the terror-ists." Closing the action, she opened the lens caps on the scope and turned each of the lenses of the LRS E-Dot to catch the light from the draftsman's lamp on the end of the bench. Even from the bed, he saw the purple optical coating on the glass.

"And?"

"And we found them. Three were still in Panama City. Panamanian Intelligence caught them in the warehouse where they'd stashed the cars. Rydell and I tracked the other two to Colón." She extended the weapon and sighted the scope through a window, then opened the battery com-partment and inserted a fresh cell. After switching the unit on, checking it again, and switching it off, she set the Contender aside and reached for the .44 barrel.

Colón was the whorehouse of Panama, the most dangerous city in the country, and her being there sucked, even with Rydell at her back.

But that was the business, and those were the jobs, and Travis knew that Panamanian Intelligence had specifically requested Gillian because they'd expected the engagement to take place in an urban setting. When there were a lot of people around on busy city streets, the shooter had to be exception-ally skilled.

El cazador espectral, ghostly hunter. That's what

the Panamanians had called the operator known as Red Dog in the beginning, because Kid Chaos Chronopolous's newest partner had those exceptional skills. As it had become known that Kid's partner was a woman, the label had changed to its feminine form, *la cazadora espectral*, which, in the Latin mind, had made her all the more terrifying.

Rightly so.

He knew for a fact, because he'd been there with her and seen her do the deed too many times not to know that when she pressed the trigger on her long rifle, she was an emotional blank. All she felt—truly *all* she felt—was recoil.

"What went wrong?"

"A prostitute," she said, doing the same check on the .44 that she'd done on the .223. "We caught the men coming out of a brothel. We knew they were in there, no surprise in Colón, and Rydell and I set up across the street in a hotel facing the house. I had the SR-25 bagged in on a table, the crosshairs on the door. Rydell was backing me up with his M-4, but when the cartel boys came out, they weren't alone."

"They had a woman with them?"

"A girl," she said, opening the lens caps on the .44's scope. "She couldn't have been more than thirteen."

That wouldn't have stopped Red Dog, if she'd had a shot.

"I took the second guy out first, then smoked the first guy."

Which was exactly what he would have expected her to do, girl or no girl.

"Rydell confirmed the hits, and we packed up and split."

"But?" There had been something.

"The girl"—she shrugged—"the girl was wearing a white dress, a summery white dress, and when I shot the man holding on to her hand, his blood got all over it. *All* over it. And she started screaming. And she kept screaming. And even after Rydell and I left the room, and left the hotel, and left freaking Colón, I could still hear her screaming in her bloody white dress."

"Can you still hear her?" he asked, keeping his voice calm, despite the sudden demoralizing dread he felt. He hated for her to suffer, and he didn't know if it would ever end. Dr. Brandt at Walter Reed held out hope, but Dr. Brandt wasn't the one who held her together in the middle of the night. He wasn't the one who helped her work through her pain. And Dr. Brandt sure as hell wasn't the one who tied her up.

Travis had a feeling the good doctor might look a little askance at that particularly intense and intensely intimate form of therapy, and yeah, he knew he was out there somewhere on a limb calling it that—but he was out there with her.

"No," she said. "It stopped about halfway back to Panama City, but..."

But he knew it scared her, the way her mind worked sometimes. Scared her that someday she might get stuck in some strange place in her head where cleaning her weapons and following orders and physically training wouldn't save her.

"I still hear you screaming sometimes," he told her. "It'll wake me up in a cold sweat, babe."

"But I'm already awake when it happens to me." She closed the lens caps on the scope and set the .44 barrel back in the case.

"I know." He'd seen her get caught in the sudden confusion and pain of a flashback. He'd seen her work to hold on to the reality of the present. If Dylan had known how often it happened, there was no way the boss of SDF would have allowed her to do the work she did. But without the work, Travis was afraid she would be completely lost. "The trauma of those kinds of experiences doesn't just go away, but no matter what happens, we'll deal with it."

Her gaze lifted from the Contender's case and met his. "You were there when I first woke up in the hospital, waiting for me, ready to hold me, ready to catch me."

"Always," he said. "And it won't change, Gillian, never." The same mix of guilt, responsibility, love, and lust that had put him by her bedside in the beginning had only grown stronger over the years, tying him to her in ways he didn't always understand, but always accepted. She was his, and there was no love without taking the responsibility that went with it.

He sure as hell could do without the guilt, though. It ate at him. He should have taken better care of her that night. He should have taken more care with her.

She started to say something, but then stopped when his phone rang.

Leaning over the side of the bed, he rummaged through his clothes until he found his cell. One look at the signal on the screen told him everything he needed to know. He immediately got up and started getting dressed.

"Who is it?"

"SDF, a call in." There wasn't a person on the other end of the line. Only the signal had been sent, but it was enough. Something was up, and Travis needed to be front and center at 738 Steele Street ASAP.

"My phone isn't ringing," she said, looking toward her fanny pack.

"Good. You need the rest." He shrugged into his shoulder holster and reached for his shoes. "If I can come back, I will. Otherwise, you know the drill."

"I'll be here."

"Good," he said, crossing the room and leaning down to give her a kiss. "I'm glad you're home, babe. I'll be back."

It wasn't until he was halfway down the outside stairs, heading for the street, that it occurred to him that with all the sex, and then more sex, he'd forgotten something very important.

He'd forgotten to ask her about El Salvador.

CHAPTER

12

His wife had the most amazing ass in the world, Dylan Hart thought, tilting his head to one side to better see through his office door, watching Skeeter bend over the computer desk in the main office on the seventh floor of Steele Street.

She did it on purpose, just for him, wearing pink fishnet hose, a little white lace miniskirt, and a pink-and-white striped bustier.

He knew it.

She knew it.

And Superman knew it.

"Cut the crap, Dylan."

"Tell her to cut it out," he said, grinning. Her hair was all piled up on top of her head in a messy ponytail twisted around and held in place with a pair of bright red chopsticks to match the skinny red patent leather belt around her waist and the red patent leather four-inch spike heels on her feet, her "catch me/fuck me" shoes.

He'd caught her a couple of times in those shoes.

He'd caught her a couple of times in nothing but those shoes.

The memory flashed, a few brain cells caught on fire and went up in smoke, and suddenly, this very important meeting he was having with Hawkins needed to come to an end.

Schooling his features, he checked his watch.

"Aren't Kat and the kids due back in a couple of minutes?" Superman was up to a brood of two, Alexandria and John Thomas Hawkins, with another one on the way.

"You're becoming dangerously transparent, Dylan."

And hot, he thought, his gaze straying back out the door.

Skeeter was being bad.

She bent deeper over the desk, widening her stance, and his imagination went into overdrive, filling in a lot of—

"Dylan?"

Details. Hot, erotic details.

"Dylan?"

Two weeks, that's how long he'd been gone. Two long, dreary weeks in London, researching a name General Grant had given him: Sir Arthur Kendryk, Lord Weymouth. It hadn't taken two weeks for Dylan to surmise that Grant was justified in being concerned about the man. Kendryk had insulated himself from the criminal elements of his organization with thousands of yards of red tape and innumerable layers of legitimate business dealings, but the ties were there. Dylan's job was going to be sorting through it all and stealing what he needed in order for Grant to be able to take his suspicions to the undersecretary of defense at the Defense Department. International arms dealing, influence peddling, and drug trafficking on the scale Kendryk seemed to be involved with posed a credible security threat to the United States.

Which meant, of course, that Skeeter's sweet ass was going to have to wait.

He leveled his gaze back at Hawkins.

"So she went to El Salvador after the Panama mission," he said, the "she" in question being the "she" who was always in question at SDF, their stringer, Red Dog. "Why?"

"The guys at the DEA say Tony Royce has opened a branch office there, in a town called San Luis. He's working with Mara Plata, using the gang as a rung of bottom-feeders to get a foothold in Central America."

"She needs to stop fucking around with Tony Royce."

Hawkins gave a short nod. "You've told her. I've told her, and sure as hell Travis has told her. But there isn't anybody in this office who doesn't know she went to Uzbekistan when Royce was trying to put together a deal with Gul Rashid—a deal that fell apart."

"We'll take Royce out when, and if, Grant tells us to take him out." Which couldn't be any too soon to suit Dylan, especially since his London trip. The whole Rashid deal was getting a lot of play in a lot of bad places, and one of the names that had gotten attached to the story belonged to a man connected to Arthur Kendryk.

Dylan hated it when his enemies started connecting to each other. It made the hair rise on the back of his neck, because if there was one thing he and Hawkins didn't believe in besides Santa Claus and the Easter Bunny, it was coincidences of any kind.

"Unless Red Dog gets to Royce first," Hawkins said. "There have been other deals she's blown for him, Dylan. At least two I can verify, and a couple of others I can't, but which seem to have her fingerprints all over them."

Shit. The woman needed to be reined in, before she did irreparable harm to herself or SDF. But no matter what she'd done or hadn't done, if it started to look like Royce was trying to flank SDF in retaliation for Red Dog's sabotage, Dylan didn't doubt that Grant would authorize the man's summary execution. It was an order Dylan would gladly carry out himself. He'd been there the night Gillian Pentycote had been tortured, and he cut her a lot of slack because of it, but there were limits.

The SDF operators were loose cannons, they were cowboys, and they were a good many other things, but they weren't out-and-out pirates. They could—and would—act when no one else seemed able to, which Dylan figured was what had prompted White Rook to sponsor an outfit like SDF in the first place, but they had a line they didn't cross, the one drawn for them by General Grant.

It was the only line they needed—most of them. Red Dog was the exception. Sometimes he wondered if there were any lines she wouldn't cross, and sometimes he wondered what he might have to do, if she went too far.

"Is Rydell still in Panama?" C. Smith Rydell could be trusted to act, to get a job done without making a mess of things or exposing SDF to unwanted scrutiny. A DEA agent for years before he'd joined the chop-shop boys on Steele Street, he knew how to cover his ass and his tracks.

"I already sent him to El Salvador. He's in San Luis tonight. I tasked him with intercepting Gillian, but he's ended up on his own. She showed up in Commerce City about two hours ago."

"Good." At least they knew where she was.

The ringing of a phone out in the main office caught his attention. The look on Skeeter's face when she answered it had him straightening up in his chair, tuned in to his wife.

She turned more fully toward him and met his gaze. After a couple of seconds, she put the caller on hold.

"You might want to take this," she said. "The call is showing FBI encryption, but it's not a government number, and the point of origin appears to be New Jersey. Atlantic City. He's asking to talk with you, personally."

"Route it through your system," he said. "Record and trace, and put it on my speaker."

She turned back to the phone in the office, and almost immediately, the "incoming" indicator lit up on his console.

"Hart," he said.

"Mr. Hart," the voice on the other end said. "My name is Ruben Setineri. I'm calling on behalf of a mutual acquaintance with information regarding the itinerary of a subject that may be of interest to you."

The man's name alone was enough to garner Dylan's undivided attention. He glanced at Hawkins, who looked equally intrigued. Ruben Setineri was a prominent, if somewhat notorious, New York attorney who represented Francis Tiburon, an East Coast mob figure.

What in the hell, Dylan wondered, would Frankie T's lawyer be doing calling this office on a secure line? The look on Hawkins's face said he was wondering the same damn thing.

"I'm listening," he said.

"I have been instructed to tell you that a Tony Royce, traveling with five companions, has boarded Frontier Airlines Flight one-twenty-one from Las Vegas to Denver," Setineri said. "The flight is scheduled to arrive an hour from now."

"I understand," Dylan said. "Anything else?"

"No," Setineri said. "Have a pleasant evening, Mr. Hart."

The indicator light winked out.

Dylan knew Skeeter had recorded the call, but he went ahead and jotted the information down on a notepad anyway.

"Talk to me," he said to Hawkins, tossing the pen aside when he was finished.

"Frankie T's got it in for Royce," his second in command said. "That's obvious. There's no other reason to give him up to us. So now we know Royce is trying to elbow his way in on Sin City's drug trade, and with his usual charm, pissing people off left and right."

"Why is he coming to Denver?"

"Because while he's been pissing off Frankie T, Red Dog has been pissing him off, and somehow, somewhere, someway while she was in El Salvador, she let him know where to find her. Knowing Gillian, it was probably by engraved invitation with a self-addressed and pre-stamped RSVP card. I'll put in another call to Smith, see if I can get through to him this time and find out what in the hell has been going on in San Luis these last four days."

"What about the FBI encryption?"

Hawkins gave him a resigned grin. "Business as usual, boss. You know it, and I know it. FBI surveillance picked Royce up in Vegas, but a hundred bucks says they don't have a warrant for him, and not enough balls to get one. The CIA has declared him strictly hands off. He's got too many 'insurance' files on too many of the people he worked with, and too many of them are too close to retirement to take a stand. So the FBI goes to the mob and gets Frankie T to give him up to us. We get the dirty work, and all the Feds get to sleep at night. Like I said, business as usual."

Yeah, that's exactly the way Dylan had figured it, too. Business as usual—totally convoluted.

"You better call Grant," Hawkins said.

"Yeah. And you call Smith."

"Roger that," Hawkins agreed. "And we're going to need—"

"Yeah," Dylan interrupted and turned in his chair to look out his office door. "Skeeter, get me Lieutenant Bradley."

"Check line two," she answered. "I've already got her on."

That was Steele Street, a well-oiled machine.

Dylan hit two. "Loretta."

"Mr. Hart," came a cool, competent female voice on the other end.

"I need a favor."

"Of course you do." She didn't sound any too happy about it, but that was just Loretta, his favorite lieutenant at the Denver Police Department. He'd been sixteen the first time she'd saved his ass, a skill she'd had plenty of opportunity to hone over the years on all the chop-shop boys.

"Flight one-twenty-one from Las Vegas is arriving at Denver International in an hour," he said. "I need surveillance on a group of passengers."

"Do you have names?"

"One. Remember Tony Royce?"

"Unfortunately, yes," she said dryly. "As a matter of fact"—he heard papers being shuffled—"I received a 'person of interest' bulletin two days ago on the ex-spook-turned-entrepreneur, one of those 'if located, do not approach, contact originating agency only' things. In this case, it's the DEA, so I'm guessing he's up to his ears in drugs."

"And other things," Dylan confirmed.

"How many people are traveling with him?"

"Five. I could use surveillance footage on all six, what kind of luggage they pick up, and what they're driving when they leave the airport. I'm going to send someone out there, now."

"I assume you don't want the Feds to know about this just yet."

"Give me what you can, Loretta, a few hours at least, and maybe I can save both of us a whole lot of trouble."

She let out a small snort. "That's not the way it usually works when SDF hits the streets, and they're my streets, Dylan, every single one. As a sworn peace officer, I'd like some assurances that you're going to keep the gunfire and body count to an acceptable level."

"What's acceptable?" He knew. She knew. And she knew he knew, because it never changed.

"Zero."

"You know I always do my best."

"Keep it contained, Dylan, and if you fail, and this thing turns violent, I expect you to let me know *before* it happens."

"Yes, ma'am."

"Give me Skeeter, then," she said. "The department still has a full-time unit of cops at DIA. They can report directly to me, and I'll transmit the footage to your office."

"Thanks, Loretta," he said. "There'll be a little something extra in your Christmas stocking this year."

A short laugh escaped her. "Make it Buck Grant, and you're going to buy yourself a whole lot of Get Out of Jail Free cards."

Buck?

"You mean General Grant?" Now she'd surprised him. "When did you meet General Grant?"

"Last week, when he was in town. Christian brought him down to the precinct."

The phone was still on speaker, and Dylan raised an eyebrow in Hawkins's direction.

Superman just shrugged.

"I showed him around a little, and we went out for drinks afterward," Loretta continued, and Dylan's eyebrow went even higher. "He's a nice guy, very cute."

Drinks with Loretta? That was bad enough, but nice? Cute?

Their older-than-dirt commanding officer?

Geezus. The guy had cut his teeth in Vietnam, running recon behind enemy lines. There was nothing "cute" about him.

"Is he single?" she asked, and Dylan got a bad feeling in his gut.

"Very," he said, maybe a little too quickly, but it was the truth. This was a nowhere, no way deal, and it had to be nipped in the bud. Richard "Buck" Grant went through women like combat soldiers went through ammo, hard and fast, and he was the last damn thing Loretta Bradley needed. SDF wouldn't be able to breathe in Denver if Buck messed around with the lieutenant.

He shot Hawkins a look that said "What in the hell were you thinking?" and Superman grinned, which just went to prove how sappy and idiotic a guy could get after three years of marriage and two kids.

"Well, if he's ever ready to be unsingle, you be sure and let me know."

"You'll be my first call."

Not.

"Thanks, Hart. Keep it safe out there tonight."

"Always, Loretta."

He turned off the call and swung around to face

Hawkins, whose smile quickly faded. There was another order of business, and it wasn't the lieutenant's love life, and they both knew it.

"You or me?" Hart asked.

"You're the only one she's afraid of," Hawkins said. "If you tell her to stand down, she might."

"Might?"

"The girl's not all there, Dylan. You know it. I know it, and she knows it."

And everybody knew why. Tony Royce could only be coming to Denver for one reason: to finish the job Dr. Souk had started two years ago. To kill Gillian Pentycote.

CHAPTER

13

TWO HUNDRED AND FIFTY thousand dollars, Smith thought, tossing the last bundle back on the bed, a quarter of a million dollars, in cash, free and easy, just lying there with all the other stuff she'd had in her tote. And he meant stuff with a capital "S," a big fricking pile of it.

He flipped his flashlight off. With the candle he'd put in the bathroom and the one he'd lit next to the bed, it was light enough for what he needed to do next without wasting any more of his batteries.

"You bastard."

She'd already said that, about half a dozen times.

"You can call me names all night long, Ms. York,

but that isn't going to change the facts." And the facts were that she was in trouble—with a capital T. A *gringa* carrying a quarter of a million in U.S. currency in Central America could only mean one of three things, none of which was a shopping spree. Ransom was the first thing that came to mind. Some relative of hers had been kidnapped, and she'd been sent to pay the ransom, for which every man in her family should be strung up. Ransom was bad, a real tragedy with lousy odds, but ransom could be the high point of this hit parade. The other two options were going to land her polka-dotted butt in jail: Either she was a money mule for some drug dealer, or she could be putting together a deal for herself. Either one would have him calling his old buddies at the DEA office in Panama City and delivering one cupcake to go.

"I'm going to give you one more chance to explain your mission of mercy. I suggest you make it good, or you're going to find yourself under arrest, and trust me, being under arrest in El Salvador is the last damn thing you want, Ms. York. They've got cockroaches bigger than you in Salvadoran jails."

Her eyes widened at that, and he made a mental note that cockroach threats worked with her.

Fuck. Cockroaches were the least of her problems.

But she didn't think so.

He could tell by the horrified look on her face.

"It's f-for the children."

Children.

Well, that was the last damn thing he'd expected, maybe even less than last.

"What children?"

"Julia's."

He didn't know what in the hell she was talking about, but somehow, it had the ring of truth. She'd brought a quarter of a million dollars into El Salvador for Julia's children.

"Who's Julia?"

"My sister, Sister Julia."

Sister, Sister Julia might have taken any other guy a while to interpret, but he'd been working the Latino beat for a long time, and nine times out of ten, the word "sister" attached to a woman's name meant one thing: nun, a Catholic angel of mercy. Bride of Christ. A habit and a rosary.

"Nuns don't have children." It was a deal breaker. He was a little low on his catechism, but he knew that much.

And her sister was a nun. There wasn't much he could do with that right off the bat. It was going to take a little getting used to, take some time to wrap his mind around even the remote possibility of somebody who looked like Honey York being a nun.

"The St. Mary's p-parish orphans," she explained. "The orphanage is old and falling apart, becoming dangerous. A month ago, one of the younger boys fell and broke his arm when part of a stair railing gave way. Julia's been lobbying the bishop for more funds, but the orphans of San Luis aren't in his budget this year, so she's taking matters into her own hands. She's going to fix the building herself, out of her trust fund."

It took a lot to make Smith blink, but trust-fund-baby brides of Christ was enough to do the job.

Geezus. Who was this woman?

He let his gaze go over her again, a little more carefully. She looked expensive. He'd noticed that on the street, but what he hadn't really had a chance to notice was just exactly how expensive.

He flicked his flashlight back on and ran the beam down her dress.

Off the rack.

Off the rack at some designer's shop was his guess. He knew what the material felt like, and he sure as hell could see what the dress fit like, and it felt and fit like couture, utter perfection in a size two petite. And those shoes—he steadied the beam on her feet. Those shoes brought only two words to mind.

Skeeter.

Bang.

Actually, Skeeter Bang Hart now, Queen of Hot Shoes, hot, expensive shoes, and the shoes Smith was looking at brought a dozen pair of Skeeter's shoes to mind: her Blahniks, running at four hundred dollars a pop, and no, he never wanted to have to explain to Dylan what he'd been doing in Dylan's wife's shoe closet with Dylan's wife for an hour.

Research would have been his first line of defense, but Smith didn't want to bet his health or his job on Dylan buying the importance of the Fucking New Guy and ex-DEA agent needing to know the difference between a pair of Manolo Blahniks and a pair of Donald Pliners. Hell, he hadn't bought it himself, but an hour in a closet with Skeeter had been nothing but fun, even if they had only talked about shoes.

Oddly enough, it had also been educational. He knew what he was looking at: dollar signs in white, handcrafted leather wrapped around a beautiful foot and a first-class, candy-apple red pedicure.

And somehow, for a guy who had never had a foot fetish before, he wanted to get his mouth on those toes. They were just so pink, and perfect, and polished, and they all but screamed "girl," and that was something he'd been without for a while, a girlfriend, a woman, in bed, on top of him, underneath him, or in a hundred other positions he could imagine without even trying.

None of which he had any business imagining with her.

But there it was, in his head now, goddammit, a whole slide show of him and the blonde.

He cleared his throat.

"So your sister, the nun, Sister Julia from St. Mary's parish, is donating a quarter of a million dollars out of her trust fund to fix the parish orphanage?"

"Yes."

"And rather than wire the money, or transfer the funds through your bank, you personally brought it in cash, in fifty-dollar bills." The most popular currency on the face of the earth, especially in the world of black money and dark deals.

"Yes."

She'd obviously missed his implication. As a matter of fact, given the earnest look on her face and the almost desperate sincerity in her voice, it had flown right over her head, which was a point in her favor, a big point, and he had to wonder if somehow he'd accidentally slipped into a Shirley Temple movie, with the orphans, and the nun, and the boy's broken arm, and her telling him about it with her green eyes all wide and imploring.

Geezus. She even looked a little like Shirley Temple, with the curls and the polka dots, if he could just get past the halter top, which her skimpy little matching jacket did nothing to cover up.

Okay, there was no getting past that halter top, or the way she filled it out. As a matter of fact, if he was being completely honest with himself, and he always was, he didn't want to get past the halter top. He wanted to get in it, which was a little more honest than maybe it was smart for him to be with himself right now.

"Why the fifties?"

"Julia said it would be easier for her to get the work done if she could hire the workmen herself and pay them in cash. So she needed small bills."

Mierda. Bull. He wasn't buying it, and Sister Julia of St. Mary's parish in San Luis, El Salvador, would have gone to the top of his "People to Investigate" list if he was still with the DEA. What he could do was turn her name over to the Panama office and let them see if drug-running nuns were going to be the next crime wave in C.A.

"That still doesn't explain why she didn't go through the bank. They would have given her all the small bills she wanted."

Honey—God, what a name—just stood there,

looking up at him, one arm wrapped around her waist. Then she took another drag off her cigarillo, and he could see her hand was still shaking.

"I can't go to jail here," she said. "Really, I can't."

Dammit. He needed to gather her up, hold on to her, anything to help her stop trembling. Something was going to shake loose if she didn't.

"Then tell me something I can believe."

"J-Julia likes to keep a low profile," she said, blowing out a cloud of smoke.

"Why?"

Another cloud of smoke preceded her reply.

"It's not always easy being a . . . a York."

Not easy having a trust fund and everything that implied about the York family and how Honey and her sister had probably grown up? He didn't think so. Being an orphan in San Luis, now that wasn't easy.

"Why?"

"We're a little . . . uh, notorious, and given Julia's . . . calling, she prefers to keep her distance from the family. I can't blame her, not really. Sometimes I'd like to get a little distance myself, but the truth is, I haven't tried very hard." Her gaze slid away. "Too spoiled, I guess."

Finally, she'd told him something he could believe, one hundred and eighty percent.

"Notorious for what?"

"There has been some, hmmm, somewhat outrageous behavior at times." She paused, took another drag off her cigarillo, then shot him a guilty glance as she blew out the smoke. "Some of it mine."

And hey, he believed that, too, another one hundred and eighty percent. She was outrageous just standing there.

"Would you care to explain that a little more clearly?"

She shook her head, and he gave her a look that said maybe she should reconsider.

Fortunately, she got the message, sort of.

"How close am I still to going to jail?"

A nice man would have told her the truth, which was "not very close."

Smith wasn't that nice.

"I saw a cockroach once in San Salvador dragging half a plantain across a cell floor."

She blanched, but wasn't buying it.

"Liar," she said.

"He was a beast, Ms. York, and I am not lying about that."

She gave a resigned sigh and tossed her hair back over her shoulder.

"Have you taken a good look at me?"

Oh, hell, yeah, and what kind of question was that?

"Fairly good," he said carefully, and now, when he really was lying through his teeth, she bought his line.

"Maybe you better look again."

Tough job, but sure, he could swing his flashlight beam over her, very slowly, one more time, starting at those candy-apple toes and sliding up those not very long, but very nice legs. Then the knees, which were nothing but sweet, and all that lovely, exposed thigh before the hem of her—

"My face, Smith. No one has been famous for their legs since Tina Turner."

Famous?

Oh, crap. He didn't want to hear that he was stuck in his room with someone famous.

He lifted the beam of his flashlight until it landed on her face.

She was cute, no doubt about it, even more than cute, but no longer that picture of elegant chic she'd presented out in front of the Palacio. With her hair falling to her shoulders in a mass of wild curls, and standing there in a cloud of cigar smoke, smelling slightly of bourbon, she did not look familiar in any way, shape, or form. He didn't know her from Adam or Eve.

"You'll have to give me a clue." God, he hoped that didn't hurt her feelings, but no matter how famous she thought she was, she was not registering anywhere on his Fame-O-Meter.

He'd seen Angelina Jolie once, in Martinique, and *she* had registered. Oh, man, had she registered.

But not this woman.

"Honoria York-Lytton," she said, taking another puff off her cigar.

Nothing. He got nothing.

"I wrote a book, and for about two minutes, it was lauded as a groundbreaking treatise for the new face of feminism."

Still nothing, except for a spike in his interest. If she was the new face of feminism, the movement was *definitely* heading in the right direction. Not that he didn't like strong, self-actualized women. He did. He just liked them better—well, hell, he just liked them better if they looked like her.

"So what happened after the first two minutes?"

"The whole thing turned to tabloid fodder, partly because I'm a York of the York-Lytton side of the family, and mostly . . . mostly because I let it, which is just *so* typical. Honestly, there's a reason Julia doesn't want anything to do with the rest of us. I tried to redeem myself by coauthoring *Women's Sexuality Under the Yoke of Twenty-first Century Political Tyranny* with my Feminist Studies professor at Harvard, Dr. Sarah Barstow, but nobody even noticed that book."

Yeah. He'd kind of missed that one, too—thank God.

"So what's the name of the book you wrote yourself?"

Another sigh left her. "You don't want to hear this."

Yes, he did. "Try me."

Another chest-heaving sigh left her, and he dutifully noted it on his very short list of the night's blessings.

"*The Sorority Girl's Guide to Self-Help Sex*," she said.

Okay.

Take a breath.

Don't grin, or God forbid, laugh out loud.

"You're kidding me."

She slanted him a narrowed glance, a very narrowed glance. "It was a best-seller."

He just bet it had been. He bet every fraternity boy from L.A. to New York had bought that one, every college boy, every high school boy, hell, every guy in America had probably bought it.

Except for him. Somehow he'd missed—

Oh, hell.

He looked at her again, and he couldn't help himself. He grinned.

"I think my little brother has a copy."

The look she gave him was pure "I told you so," which only made his grin wider.

"You're good," he said. "You are very, very good, and I almost believed you. The whole nun thing is classic, and the orphanage is a really nice touch, but by God, *The Sorority Girl's Guide to Self-Help Sex* puts you in a class all by yourself."

She'd had him going there for a minute. He hated to admit it, but it was true. Something about her just made a guy want to believe she was telling the truth. It was a special something all the best liars had.

"Are you calling me a liar?"

He hated doing it, honest he did, but reality had a way of biting a guy in the butt if he tried to duck from it.

"In spades," he said.

Another cloud of smoke came his way. Then she turned and bent over the bed—a second notation on his list of the night's blessings.

After a few seconds of rummaging around through her stuff, she turned back to him and handed him a book: *The Sorority Girl's Guide to Self-Help Sex.*

Written by Honoria York-Lytton.

With her photograph on the back.

Fuck.

And he *really* meant it this time.

CHAPTER
14

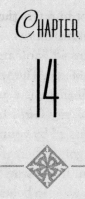

GILLIAN PENTYCOTE. Royce repeated the name in his mind for about the hundredth disbelieving time, flipping through the thick sheaf of papers Zane had handed him when they'd first gotten on the plane. It took a hell of a lot to shock him, but the information in the papers had done it.

She'd survived.

Not only had she survived, against all odds; she'd thrived.

His man had worked fast and unearthed an amazing amount of data between the time Royce had given the order for Denver and when they'd left for the airport. He had names, dates, times, places, blood tests, and psych reports. He even had her goddamn address, complete with a map marked with the route from the airport to her apartment in Commerce City.

Geezus. Under any other circumstances than what he'd found in the papers, the girl would have been breathing her last.

Beast with a brain, that was the summation of Zane Lowe's resume, but the man had truly outdone himself this time. "Red Dog" in and of itself had offered damn little in comparison to "Red Dog 303." Tying the for-hire sniper to Special Defense Force in Denver had been the key. Locking in on her home ground had opened up her past like Pandora's box.

And what a past.

Royce seldom felt excitement, but the information in the papers had lit him up. Millions of dollars were at stake, and nothing excited him more than money. One other thing came close, but now that the whole goddamn world had been handed to him on a platter, he was going to have to forgo his previous plans. There would be no pretty Thai syringe in Red Dog's immediate future, no woman screaming her heart out for him, and no Zane with his knives.

Women and knives, it was such a cliché, and yet there was something in the purely predictable outcome of that particular combination that never failed to make his blood run hot.

But not tonight.

He'd been handed the future, and its name was Red Dog, case number WR8864XS, the bitch formerly known as Gillian Pentycote—and he'd done that for her. He'd made her what she was, a warrior of world renown.

And if he'd made one, he could make another.

A smile curved his mouth, an actual goddamn smile.

Red Dog. Red Dog. He'd let the name eat at him over the course of the last two months. He'd dwelled on the death of the shadow called Red Dog, turned it over in his mind, devised it and revised it for maximum effect, and now he'd changed his mind. He wasn't going to kill her.

He was going to dissect her—piece by careful piece, never taking too much of her at a time. She'd be alive. There was no reason for her to die for a long, long time. He and his Thai medical staff could keep her breathing for as long as they needed.

Tissue samples, that's all they'd take.

And blood.

And maybe a few microscopically thin slices of her brain.

He was the one who had chosen the XT7 for her that night two years ago. Dr. Souk had laid out a whole array of psychopharmaceuticals and at one point offered the tray to him. Hart, he knew, had been given NG4, so he'd chosen one of the blue syringes, the XT7.

And look what it had done.

He turned to page seventeen of the sheaf of papers, the beginning of the medical report Zane had coerced out of a source Royce had cultivated years ago at Walter Reed Medical Center, report number WR8864XS.

The little piece of auburn-haired fluff had been turned into a killing machine—hard, fast, ruthless, skilled, expensive.

Geezus. If that's what XT7 had done to Gillian Pentycote, think what he could get by starting with better base stock. Someone like Skeeter Bang would become unstoppable, superhuman.

They'd have to run tests, check dosages, collate results. They'd need test subjects, but human life could be had pretty damn cheaply in Southeast Asia, especially women—and he needed women.

He'd watched Dr. Souk administer XT7 to men a number of times on the island of Sumba, under Hamzah Negara's watchful eye—and they'd gotten much of the same response as with the NG4 and the XXG2. Some guys died, some guys didn't; they'd all suffered profoundly for a long, long time.

But no superheroes had come out of the mix.

He looked around the plane, at the five men sitting closest to him.

Thugs. There was no other word for them. Even Zane was a thug at heart, but for the right price, they were his thugs, strong, solid, dangerous, perverse, and reliable.

But women. Hell. One of the things Royce hated about them was their faithless, twisted hearts. He also hated their goddamn unpredictability. He hated having their goddamn emotional presence anywhere in his life, and he didn't even want to think about their physical presence, other than to unequivocally categorize their bodies as vile.

And now he needed one of the goddamn things. He needed Red Dog alive, at least for a while. She still owed him for Uzbekistan. He wouldn't forget, and once he got everything out of her he needed, he'd kill her. Of course, by then, she'd probably be begging him to kill her—which meant that one way or the other, even if it took months longer than he'd anticipated, he was going to get everything he wanted.

Life was good.

CHAPTER

15

GILLIAN KNELT on the roof of a warehouse a block away from the SDF garage, hidden in the shadows, watching the night. A storm was moving in from the north. The temperature had dropped, and the wind was blowing softly against her face, the air cooling her skin.

Five and a half minutes, that's what it had taken for her to scale the three-story building with a friction loop she'd slipped around a downspout.

Her adrenaline must be up, she thought. It usually took her six.

She'd chosen her IFP, Initial Firing Position, to align herself between an air-conditioning unit on the northwest corner of the warehouse's tarred roof and her front door, where Royce's men would probably show up first. Dressed in a pair of sleek black leather pants and a black shrink shirt, with an olive green assault vest over the top, she was invisible in the urban landscape—and so she would remain, all night long.

She had a gift for stealth. It was her most valuable tactical skill, the ability to acquire a target, move undetected into position, make the kill, and evaporate into thin air. It was what had made her reputation, what had made her second life possible.

But her second life was coming to an end. She felt it with each passing day. Something was happening to her, something to do with the XT7. The incidents with her arm were increasing in frequency. The flashbacks to the night in the white room were crashing in on her more and more often.

She wasn't going to make it through to a better end. She knew that now, had known it for weeks, but she wasn't going out alone. She was taking Tony Royce with her—one way or the other. That was the bitch in her, demanding justice, demanding revenge, but God, it was costing her.

She slipped her hand inside her assault vest and pressed it against her sternum, trying to ease the ache she'd had since she'd left her loft. It was just her breath, caught in a stream of regret—she knew that. Just her heart realizing what she'd done.

Angel . . . she'd let him go.

For the last time.

So it was, and so it had to be.

But God, it hurt.

Rising to her feet, forcing herself to focus on the mission, she slid her hand deeper into her vest and checked her gear. The Contender with its fourteen-inch .223 barrel was loaded and secure in a holster on the inside left panel of the vest. The .44 barrel assembly was in a sleeve sewn into the inside right panel. Her initial ammo supply for the weapon was in the cartridge cuff cinched around her right forearm—ten rounds of .223 and five rounds of subsonic .44.

The warehouse was an excellent shooting platform for the long-range pistol. A low wall around the rooftop gave her perfect cover. The corners had one-foot-square cutouts, designed to allow water to run off into the downspouts, and she knew if she dropped flat, each one would give her a protected, narrow line of sight to a section of the outlying area. She could make a shot through one of the cutouts and remain concealed and covered from return fire.

Such had her life become. The only life she knew: concealment, cover, taking the shot, making the kill, egress. There had been something else before, something softer, more emotionally complex.

Without Angel, she feared she might feel nothing at all. He was the touchstone, the path—and he was gone.

A short, sharp breath left her, sudden, unexpected, a sign of pain. Her hand went back to the middle of her chest, and she pressed again, easing away the ache, and when it was gone, she let it all go.

There was no other way.

She had her mission and thirty pounds of gear to achieve the night's two objectives: Kill Royce; survive.

There was nothing else.

The TC Contender inside her vest was a purely offensive weapon. For defense, she had her .40 caliber long-slide Glock holstered on her hip and two hundred rounds of ammunition in her magazines and stowed in her pack. And if things really didn't go her way, she had a Tanto combat knife in an upside-down sheath secured to the front of her vest. Even if it came to a knife fight, though, she wouldn't count herself out. She'd been taught by the best, Creed Rivera.

Creed had taught her a lot of things, and warned her about others—*Take care, Roja, Red . . . take care that you do not become what you're sworn to destroy. There is a damn thin line between darkness and evil.*

Razor thin. She knew the importance of taking care. He'd made damn sure she knew. He'd lectured her, backed her up against a wall and gotten in her face one night when he'd thought she'd come too damn close to going too damn far. No one at Steele Street walked the edge of darkness more carefully or with a surer step than Creed. No one else needed to, and he understood that about himself. He understood it about her, too.

Take care, Roja, or you'll be lost.

"I'm already lost," she'd told Travis later.

"Not in that way," he'd said. "We all work close to the line, but we're still the good guys, Gillian. Creed knows how easy it would be to take the last step, and he knows there isn't any coming back from it. Once you cross over that way, you're his enemy. You'll be your enemy, too. You'll be what Royce has become."

It happened in their business, more often than anyone official would ever admit: trained operatives turning rogue, going for the money, or for the glory that was no longer legally sanctioned to be theirs. They got old, they got hurt, they got kicked off whatever team they'd given their life to, and some of them turned. The skills they had were a valuable commodity on the world stage, and crime paid top dollar to get them.

Royce had been so successful; he was almost the

exception to the rule. He didn't work for an underworld crime lord; he was an underworld crime lord.

She was doing the right thing.

Killing Royce was the right thing, not just for herself, but for everybody.

If she'd doubted it, even for a second, she wouldn't have been standing on a rooftop alone, wishing for things she couldn't have, that life had been different, that Angel was with her.

Swearing under her breath, she wiped the back of her hand across her cheek. It came away wet.

Geezus. She couldn't be crying. Red Dog didn't even know how to cry.

CHAPTER 16

SHE WAS ON her second bottle of booze.

He was on his first.

Smith looked at the shot's worth of gin in the tiny bottle in his hand. She'd kept the bourbon for herself. She'd said gin made her excitable, whatever the hell that meant, and he'd agreed that maybe it was better if she didn't get too excited.

They had enough excitement.

It was a funny thing about explosions. People knew they were dangerous, but that didn't send them running in the other direction for very damn long. Within minutes after the explosion over by the marina, people had started flooding into the streets, most definitely getting in the way of the emergency response crews, and as of a few minutes back, maybe starting to riot.

Standing off to the side of the broken windows, he twisted the lid off the tiny bottle of gin and watched a group of young men gathering in front of the cantina across the street. It wasn't full out yet, not even close, but the crowd was shifting, and he was expecting it to be one damn long night. One damn long night trapped in a hotel room with Honoria York-Lytton.

He glanced back toward the bed, and his gaze slid over her, top to bottom.

Excitement. Right. He wasn't too worried about an ounce of gin getting him going, but the odds were growing damn short on the polka-dot dress since she'd taken off her jacket.

There was no back to the dress. None. It was open clear to her waist. The straps of the halter top buttoned at the back of her neck, very classy, two red buttons that were the same size and color as the polka dots. He guessed you could call it camouflage, sorority girl camouflage.

Yeah, a person could call it something all right. *Geezus.* He grinned. No wonder the family nun had run away.

Red Dog would have called the buttons too damn cute, which wasn't exactly a compliment coming from the bad girl. But Red Dog was all edge, a sharp, dark edge, and Honey—God, he had to love that name—Honey was all curves, one right after another, all of them sliding together inside that dress where she was sitting in the middle of his bed going through her pile of junk.

Kee-rist. He tossed half the contents of the little bottle back, then finished it with another swallow and looked down at the book in his other hand— and he grinned again. It was impossible not to.

The Sorority Girl's Guide to Self-Help Sex—with her photograph on the back.

His grin broadened.

He knew a little about self-help sex. Some months he knew a little more about it than he liked to admit. He even knew a little about sorority girls, but none of the ones he'd ever dated had looked like Honey. They'd been college girls back when he'd been a college boy, and Honey York was no girl. Age-wise, she was nearing perfection, which in his book meant somewhere over thirty. There was something about women's bodies as they got older, a certain lushness that a guy could really get lost in, which was reason enough in his book to let women over thirty rule the planet. God knew, he'd been ruled by a few, even a couple when he'd been in his twenties, and one when he'd been nineteen, and yeah, that had been a real education. He still kept in touch with Caroline.

But it had been a while since he'd been in touch with any woman.

His last girlfriend had left without a forwarding address when he'd missed one too many flights home to Denver. Work had kept coming up in Central America, and he'd kept taking it. That was the way it was with guys like him. No commitment. No hard feelings. And eventually, no girlfriend.

The pattern had never failed him.

He wondered what Honey's story was, if she was as single as she looked. There was no triple-digit-carat ring on her finger, and she still had the family name—and here came his reality check: Those were probably the only two things they had in common. He wasn't married, and he hadn't yet disgraced himself so badly that the old man had disowned him. Not hardly. A policeman in Little Rock, Arkansas, Jack Rydell was damned proud of his oldest son. The admiration went both ways.

"I don't know how you missed me," Honey said, continuing their conversation after taking a moment to unbuckle the ankle straps on her shoes and slip them off her feet. "I was on the cover of *Ocean* magazine, and on the front page of every tabloid in America for three months, with headlines like *Shameless Sorority Sex Games*."

He didn't know how to tell her that he'd never heard of *Ocean* and didn't spend much time reading the tabloids, but he couldn't deny that if he'd seen it, *Shameless Sorority Sex Games* might just have been his ticket into dropping a couple of bucks on a grocery store rag.

"I've been out of the country quite a bit this last year." And the year before that, and the year before that.

"The book really isn't about sex games."

And this was practically a fantasy come true, to have a hot, barefoot blonde in his bed, talking about sex games.

"And it's *not* about masturbation. I got a lot of that, because of the title."

O-kay. They were headed into *serious* fantasyland now.

He looked at the empty bottle in his hand, wondered if she had another, and decided he'd probably had enough. No matter what she ended up talking about, he had a job to do, which was to get the two of them through to sunrise, which, as long as they stayed put in the Palacio, shouldn't be too damned difficult, especially since she was no longer the focus of anyone's attention. Everyone had moved on to explosions and street action, and moved away from slightly notorious, but not very famous, tawny-haired blondes.

"The publisher picked the title, not me. If you look at the chapter headings, you'll see what the book is really about."

He'd get right on that, sure, as soon as he figured out what all those young men were up to over at the cantina. They were starting to mill around and band together, to form up.

Trouble, he decided a moment later, when he saw an AK-47 snugged up against one guy's body.

He started across the room, heading for the large chest of drawers pushed against one of the walls.

"Slip your shoes back on and get over here," he said, getting her *out* of his bed, which was just plain stupid. But he needed her. "Help me with this."

He didn't care how cute she was; when men started showing up with AKs, everyone had to pull their weight.

Or not, he realized a moment later, after he'd directed her to one side of the chest he wanted to move in front of the broken windows. The chiffonier was pure jungle hardwood, and big, which made it perfect, and perfectly heavy.

Too heavy for Honey to even give it a budge.

"Are you back there?" he asked, dragging the damn thing across the floor, but not feeling much push with his pull.

"*Yes,*" she gasped, and he looked around the

edge of the chest to see if she was okay, and immediately felt foolish.

Hell. He'd been spending too much time with Red Dog. That girl could have moved a jungle hardwood chiffonier with her will and one damn cold look from those spooky golden eyes.

Honey couldn't have moved it with a crane. But it was cute to see the way she'd put her shoulder into it, and how the position curved her back and made her butt stick out, and how it made her dress ride up, and how she planted her platformed feet to give herself some leverage.

"You don't work out much, do you." It wasn't a question.

"Not . . . much," she admitted, gritting her teeth and still pushing for all she was worth.

Halfway across the room, she changed positions, putting her back into it, not that it made a damn bit of difference. She wasn't complaining, though, and he appreciated it, and she didn't give up, which impressed him. Trying that hard and being totally ineffective would have depressed the hell out of him. He expected results from everything he did, whatever it was, and he got them, every time.

So he pulled, and the damn thing moved, inch by inch, until he got it situated in front of the windows. The instant he stopped pulling, he realized his mistake.

He heard the plop of her butt hitting the floor just half a second before he heard her cry out.

"Oh, *ow*."

"Sorry." He should have warned her.

"Oh, *ow*. Oh, I . . . oh, *ow*. I—"

Then it hit him like a train wreck. *Shit*.

"Don't move," he said, stepping around the chiffonier and kneeling down next to her. Sure enough, she was sitting in broken glass.

"*Owww*." The word came out real soft and real slow, like it really, really hurt. Then she looked up at him, and he could tell it hurt. Her face was sort of scrunched up, and she was holding herself really still. "Oh, Mr. Smith, I-I . . . *ow*."

"No Mr., remember, just Smith, and don't move. Just let me pick you straight up."

"M-my shoes slipped."

Of course, they had.

He slid one arm under her knees and the other around her back.

Her bare back.

Without hesitation, her arms went around his neck, and as carefully as possible, he shifted his weight and scooped her up—and she melted into him.

It was amazing.

It was the softest lamination of his life. Every curve she had found a place on his body and molded itself to him.

"*Ow*," she said again, real soft again, her voice little more than a sigh against the side of his neck, her breath blowing along the edge of his ear.

Sex.

It was the only thought he had for a couple of eternal seconds, during which he didn't move, just stood there like a pole-axed idiot and thought sex. Nothing specific, just sex, the whole thing.

"I-I think I've got glass in my butt."

Yeah, he was pretty sure she did, too.

And he had nothing for brains. He was running on empty, which was just about the stupidest damn thing that had ever happened to him—getting pole-axed by a woman named Honey in a polka-dot dress with glass in her butt.

CHAPTER
17

"GET A ROPE ON HER," General Richard "Buck" Grant growled over the phone, and Dylan couldn't help but agree. It was a damn good idea.

"We're on it, sir." Or as "on it" as he could get at the moment. Steele Street was a little short-handed. Hawkins had left for the airport. Skeeter was manning the communications, and he was taking orders and gearing up to ask a favor. This shit with Royce had gone on long enough.

Too long, actually. Dylan didn't give a damn whose career was hanging in the balance over at the CIA. He didn't give a damn how much dirt Royce had on some of those higher-echelon types, or who needed the asshole alive. He hadn't cared in two years, not since Royce had revealed himself as a traitor. He wanted the man dead.

But except for one small window of opportunity directly after the night Gillian Pentycote had been abducted, when Royce had been fair game, Dylan's hands had been tied. Tony Royce was off limits, on orders of someone he didn't dare cross. The price for disobedience was the existence of SDF. Dylan didn't know who had put the pressure on White Rook to draw SDF off Royce's trail, but he knew that if they didn't obey the command, Rook could and would bury the whole team and shut down 738 Steele Street so tight it would take a presidential order for the place to ever see the light of day again.

The party would be over.

Dylan knew it. Grant knew it. And Red Dog knew it. Dylan had been very clear on the subject.

" 'On it' isn't good enough, Dylan. I don't want to lose her because of goddamn Tony Royce, not when we should have taken him out years ago," Grant said. "But if she's lured him to Denver and is out there gunning for him, then we've got a rogue operator on our hands, and the shit will hit the fan all the way to the Potomac. If she can't put the welfare of the team ahead of her personal problems, I can't protect her, and neither can you. Do you understand?"

"Yes, sir." He did. He understood perfectly. "I won't know for sure what happened in El Salvador until we make contact with Rydell."

"Then do it."

"We're trying."

"Do better than try. If she wasn't within a thousand miles of Royce's place in San Luis, and it's just one big, goddamn coincidence that the two of them are ending up in Denver on the same goddamn night after a little sojourn in El Salvador, well, then we've got nothing to worry about. What about her? Have you been able to contact her yet?"

"No. Skeeter has tried her cell a number of times, but Red Dog isn't answering or returning calls," Dylan said. "Can you contact White Rook? See what he can get us. Authorization to kill Royce and anyone in his employ would cover Red Dog's ass."

There was a moment of silence.

"And yours. You know it's never been that simple, and it's no simpler now than the last ten times you've asked for the same goddamn thing."

"This is different. He's here, and he's a threat to one of our contractors."

"And as always, you are within your rights to take appropriate exigent measures to neutralize an emergent threat."

"Screw 'emergent.' I want the right to track him

down and kill him, Buck." There was more to it than Gillian, a lot more. Royce had been after him the night she'd been abducted. He'd been behind Dylan's kidnapping and subsequent torture in Indonesia, and Royce had been SDF's CIA contact for the mission that had gotten J.T. Chronopolous killed.

They all wanted him dead for that.

"I've put two calls in since we started this conversation, Dylan, and if I can get you a finding to sanction his termination, no one will be happier than me. Who's with you in the Bat Cave tonight?"

"Hawkins is on his way to the airport. He's going to tail Royce into town, see where the bastard lights, and Skeeter is here."

"I thought Chronopolous and James were back from Thailand today."

"Kid stayed in Los Angeles. His wife is having a showing of her work there."

"She paints naked men, right?"

"Uh . . . right." Dylan guessed that was one way to sum up a singularly brilliant career in fine art.

"Never did understand that," Grant said. "Naked women I could understand. But men . . . hell, who wants to look at a bunch of—hell, whatever. What about Travis James?"

"He's my next call. Chances are, he's with Gillian."

"Then we don't have a problem. Right? Travis can keep her under control."

"Right." At least he hoped to hell he was right. Red Dog and the Angel Boy had a connection that—hell, that Dylan wasn't sure he understood, or that he even wanted to understand. She was a hard woman. She'd push any guy, and any guy besides Travis James would probably get pushed too far.

But Travis was different from all the other hard-ass chop-shop boys. He'd been a silver-spoon Boulder slacker-dude, majoring in feminist studies and conflict resolution, or some such damn thing, before he'd come on board at SDF. He more than carried his weight on the team, or Creed would have lost him in the jungle a long time ago, but the guy couldn't port a head or bolt ten pounds of boost onto a car—any car. Dylan wasn't sure Travis knew how to change the oil in a car—any car. He drove a crapped-out Jeep that Quinn wouldn't even let him park on the second floor where Quinn kept his Camaros.

And he meditated. Full-out. Dylan had seen him do it, in a goddamn Lotus position no less, wrapped up like a freaking pretzel.

And he posed nude for Kid's wife, Nikki, completely bare-assed nude, sometimes wearing angel wings, sometimes bound and gagged for hours on end, and he did it without an ounce of self-consciousness or panic, and he brought that same level of coolness under pressure to his job at Steele Street.

The guy was fucking imperturbable.

It's why he had a job at Steele Street, that and the fact that he could shoot, the fact that he would and did shoot. Nothing about the man had surprised Dylan more than his willingness to kill when it was required, without hesitation and with the skills to hit who he aimed at, every time—and it was always a "who" when it counted, never a "what." Range practice was great. Dylan was all for it, but if a guy couldn't hit a target that was looking back at him, he was worthless. Less than worthless. He was a danger to his team.

"Get on the horn," Grant said. "Make sure he's with her, and when you get ahold of Rydell, let me know what the hell is going on."

"Yes—" Dylan looked up as the door to the office opened.

Fuck.

They were in trouble. Big trouble.

"—sir," he finished and hung up the phone, then watched the night head toward hell in a handbasket as Travis walked in and gave Skeeter a big hug.

He didn't mind the hug. Hell, no. But Travis was alone, and he for damn sure minded that.

Gillian was on her own, on the loose, and the only thing that could save her butt now was C. Smith Rydell. They needed a situation report on what had happened in El Salvador and how much trouble she'd really started. Smith had been in San Luis all day, so why in the hell hadn't he checked in with Superman? Just what in the hell was he doing down there?

CHAPTER

18

HOLDING HIS BREATH.

Smith was holding his goddamn breath.

He never held his breath. Ever.

But he'd never held the hem of a polka-dot dress in his fingers either, not with the intention of lifting it up and over what he knew deep in his heart was going to be a world-class ass.

Geezus.

She was face down on the bed, her junk pushed to one side, her shoes about half falling off her feet, with a truly heart-wrenching combination of silent sobs and not so silent hiccups percolating out of her.

Fuck. He had to be on *Candid Camera*. This did *not* happen to him. Ever.

"That last one hurt."

Yeah, it had hurt him, too, to pull a shard of glass out of her.

"That's the last of the big ones."

Big ones, *geezus*. They hadn't been that big, just big enough to cut her dress and stick a bit of sharp edge in her skin. There was a little blood, though.

Lucky for her, he had a Medkit. Right. Like they were going to need that.

"I think there's more in there. It still hurts. Really bad."

Yes. He ran the beam of his flashlight over her again. Her dress was pretty cut up, and he was sure there was more in there, too, which was why he was going to take a look.

"I'm going to take a look," he said in the most professional voice he could muster.

He *was* a professional, a professional soldier, not a medic. But he'd had training for situations like this, medical situations. Remaining calm was paramount.

So he was calm—until he lifted her dress, and then, for a second or two, he was a little less than calm.

She wasn't wearing underwear—that was his first impression. Then he realized she was. It was just so incredibly sheer as to be almost invisible. If it hadn't been for the tiny edge of pink lace trim, he might not have seen it at all.

It was so sheer, it didn't have a color. It was like looking at her ass through a film of water, and he could have been happy looking at it for a long, long time. But he was on a mission. He had a job to do, and in order to do it, he had to remove that sheer nothing whisper of what could only be silk.

"I don't work for the State Department." God knew why he felt compelled to tell her that.

"I know," she said, her voice muffled from where she had her face buried in her hands and in the bed.

"But I am with the U.S. government, working out of the, uh, Department of Defense."

"That's . . . that's very comforting," she said. "To know it's an actual representative of the United States government who's officially going to be taking off my underwear and looking at me naked in bed, while I lie here helplessly without my gun."

"I'm not giving your gun back." Or the bullet. It was in his pocket, a keepsake of what was turning out to be one of the craziest nights of his life. He had his limits, and arming a cupcake was beyond them. And whether she wanted to admit it or not, she had to know that the actual taking off of the underwear was completely beside the point. She was naked, right now.

"It is under only the most awful duress that I am allowing you to do this."

"It's the wise choice, Ms. York." Just slightly better than hanging around the rest of the night and letting little shards of glass work their way deeper under her skin.

Which, honestly, is what he would have done. He didn't know where her threshold of pain was, but it seemed to be set at "not very damn much." He wouldn't have stretched himself out naked on a bed for a stranger.

Except for someone like her.

Yeah, someone like her probably could talk him into it without having to talk too damn much.

Geezus. He was such a guy.

"Ms. York-Lytton to you," she said, her face still in her hands, and another small sob escaped her, followed up by a catch in her breath.

"Let's just take a look," he said, ready to do the deed and get it over with.

He slipped his fingers under the top edge of her panties, taking hold of that tiny strip of pink lace and stretching it out enough to pull everything off her without rubbing against her skin.

And the instant he bared her bottom, he realized his mistake.

"Okay," he said, keeping his voice calm. "There is another piece in there, right next to where I took the last one out, but don't worry. It'll just take a minute to remove, and then you'll be fine."

And she would be, once he got it out—but *geezus.*

He finished pulling her underwear down, but not off. He stopped at the top of her thighs, which gave him all the access he needed.

Not all he wanted, he silently admitted, and he wasn't very happy about having to admit anything. But all he needed.

She sobbed again, and yeah, he could imagine it did hurt like hell. A long sliver of glass had embedded itself under her skin, a two-inch sliver with just its tip showing.

No wonder he hadn't seen it, and no wonder she was crying and letting him take her panties off.

Which, for all the wonder of that, made him feel like shit.

He was going to have to use his knife.

"Would you like some pain meds? I have some in my pack."

"Oh, right, like I'm . . . like I'm going to take drugs from a stranger. I don't even know your name."

"Smith," he told her again.

She said something to that, something mumbled into her hands, and he thought it was "bullshit." As a matter of fact, he was pretty damn sure

that's what she'd said. Two minutes ago, it would
have made him grin, but not when he was going to
have to cut her. The sliver of glass was just under
her skin. He could see it very clearly.

"Just do it," she said, sounding completely resigned and completely miserable. "Just do what
you need to do to get it out."

Okay.

He knelt by the side of the bed, where he'd left
his pack, and pulled out his Medkit.

"Do you have another bottle of alcohol?" he
asked.

The question got another sob and some rustling
around through her junk. After a few seconds, she
lifted a little bottle over her head.

"Vodka, the good stuff. Great. Thanks." He was
rambling, and that was a first, too. He opened the
kit and pulled out some gauze bandages. Then he
pulled his folding knife out of his pocket and
thumbed it open.

"I-I heard that," she said, lifting her head out of
her hands and looking over her shoulder at him—
her bare shoulder. Her face instantly fell. "A knife?"

"I'm going to need to make a small incision," he
said, and she started to tremble.

Just like that.

Like somebody had plugged her in.

"Do you want to reconsider the meds?" he asked.

She shook her head.

"You have about a three-inch sliver of glass just under the skin. I'm going to make a small incision at the top of it and—"

"N-no."

"No?" What did she mean no?

"I want a doctor."

As if to punctuate his next thought, another explosion sounded out on the streets of San Luis, coming from the east. Not close, just close enough to be heard for what it was: trouble.

"No," he said. There was no doctor in her future, not tonight. It wasn't going to happen. "It's just a long sliver, Ms. York-Lytton. I'm not a doctor, but I have had some training, and I have taken care of much worse wounds than this without losing anybody." There had been a night up on the Rio Putumayo when his partner, Kid Chaos Chronopolous, had been hurt real bad, a couple of gunshot wounds and various other superficial traumas, not to mention they'd had to swim the friggin' Putumayo to catch a boat, and he'd gotten Kid through that just fine.

A terrible, ragged sigh left her, and she buried her face back into her hands.

"Just do it," she said, the words barely audible.

"Can you stop shaking?" His knife was razor sharp, and he'd just as soon not end up autographing her butt with it.

"No."

"Breathe."

"I *am* breathing."

Hell. He'd known it was a long shot.

"C. Smith Rydell," he said. "And that's the truth, the whole truth."

And that got her attention.

She turned to look over her shoulder.

"C. Smith Rydell?"

"Yes," he said, and handed her the flashlight. "Shine this on your butt—as best you can."

"With two *L*s?"

"Two." He poured vodka on a piece of gauze and very carefully wiped it over her skin. Then he poured a bit on the edge of his knife.

"What's the C stand—*ahh*." She gasped, but it was done.

He took the flashlight from her so she could bury her face back in her hands and cry a little. There was blood, but he got the glass out, and washed out the wound, and used a towel he'd brought from the bathroom to keep from getting the bed wet, and she sobbed a little more, and then a little more.

And he did what he did best—evaluate situations and solve problems.

He started by brushing off the rest of her butt, and yes, that was a medical procedure, using the pads of his fingers to carefully feel for more glass.

There was none—and yes, she had an incredible ass, one he wasn't likely to forget, not in his current life, and probably not in the next one, either. But all told, she'd gotten the two minor pieces and the one big sliver in her, and her amazingly flimsy dress and almost nonexistent underwear had saved her from the rest.

Satisfied, at least in one sense of the word, he put some antibiotic cream on her and bandaged her up with a folded piece of gauze and a few strips of surgical tape, and was careful not to run his fingers over the tape any more than necessary. And there it was: her ass, soft curves, incredible skin, a tan line that could only be called Brazilian—which gave him another crazy, hot thought—and a small square of perfectly white gauze.

It was amazing really, the turns a life could take. Five days ago, he'd been in another hotel room with another woman, in another Central American city: Colón, Panama.

He tilted his head to one side, surveying his handiwork for about half a second before he let his gaze drift lower, into the shadowy area between her legs. He couldn't see anything. He'd been too careful with her underwear, only pulling them down the absolute minimum amount he needed to get the job done.

Another inch would have been great.

Another two, and he'd probably have gotten himself in trouble.

He'd seen Red Dog in her underwear, her work underwear, which could best be described as sports underwear. Still, she looked damn good in it. The girl was ripped.

But there was nothing about Red Dog in her underwear that broke his heart. Sometimes he got a little turned on. She was gorgeous, and gorgeously fucked-up, but she didn't really flip his switches.

Cupcake did.

He tilted his head the other way, and wondered if there was any way on earth to have her tonight. He was already about half hard, and there wasn't much he wouldn't give to play a few rounds of Shameless Sorority-Girl Sex Games with her—the more shameless the better.

"Y-you're staring at my ass," she said, and hic-cupped.

"No, I'm not," he lied.

He saw her wipe at her tears before she turned

her head to look at him. He met her gaze straight on, without an ounce of guilt.

"Yes, you are."

In Colón, he'd watched Red Dog take out two bad guys, smoke them right on the street.

The only person getting slain here tonight was him.

"Your underwear has to go, probably the dress, too," he said. "Or at least you have to take them off long enough for me to shake them out and make sure there isn't any more glass in them."

Practicality was practically his middle name, and his suggestion was purely practical. The by-product of so much practicality—having her completely naked in his bed—really wasn't part of the equation. Really, it wasn't. His heart couldn't take it, not if he couldn't have her.

"I have some clothes you can wear," he added, and when she warily dropped her gaze down the length of him, he added a little more. "Clean clothes."

He had a camera in his pack. He just wished to hell he had the balls to use it, because he was never going to see the likes of her again. There was a reason she'd been on the cover of a magazine, and he didn't think it was just because she'd written a book.

He'd been calling her cute, and in a way, he'd

been right. He'd been thinking she was the poster girl for the ditzy blondes of the world, and in a way, he was probably a little bit right about that, too.

But looking at her now, in the Palacio, by candlelight, with a piece of gauze on her butt, bourbon on her breath, and an AK-47 chattering on the street, he knew there was more.

He knew it down to his bones.

The look she was giving him was so considering, so clear, so utterly guileless, it unnerved the hell out of him. Whatever she was seeing in him, he had a feeling it was way too much. He was a guy with secrets he kept, and she was taking off his top layer with her green-eyed gaze.

"I'll put the clothes in the bathroom. You can go in there." Maybe a little distance wasn't such a bad idea. She wasn't going anywhere out of the bathroom. The window was high and small.

Not that it was his job to contain her.

He just wanted to contain her. Keep her out of trouble. Make sure she was safe. Take her to bed.

Right.

He just wanted to keep her in sight until he could get her on a plane out of El Salvador, and whether she knew it or not, or wanted to accept it or not, that's exactly what she needed to do: Get out.

"You haven't stolen my money."

"No."

God, did she have any idea what she looked like? Raised up a little on one side to better see him, her dress pushed up around her waist, her shoes falling off, her hair completely wild, and her panties down around her thighs, not even the word "sex" quite covered it.

"And you didn't manhandle my butt."

"No." He was a professional, and he was always in control, especially of himself. Without fail. Always. No matter what he was thinking. Guys like him survived by being in control, and if they ever lost it, they survived by taking it back, hard and fast and with whatever amount of force necessary. It was jungle law, and it was ingrained in him down to the cellular level. Go, fight, win—every time.

Sure, he had a helluva imagination. But he never let it get in the way of reality, or of his being in control.

Great. He was so glad he had all that completely straight in his head. Now all he had to do was take his eyes off her.

"Why are you here?" he asked, still holding her gaze, holding it steady, like a rock.

"Because she's mine. Since the day she was born, she's been mine."

Her sister.

"Sister Julia."

She nodded.

"Your bio on the book jacket says besides a sister, you have four brothers. Why didn't one of them bring the money?"

"Because El Salvador doesn't have a club scene."

"That's cold."

"That's true."

"And she really is a nun?"

She nodded again.

"And there really are orphans?"

"Yes."

He believed her.

Hell. He let his gaze slip past her to the bundles of money piled on the bed. *Dammit.*

Reaching down into his pack, he pulled out his extra pair of cargo pants and his second-favorite parrot shirt, the green one.

"Go get dressed," he said, tossing the clothes on the bed. "And when you're decent, we'll talk."

CHAPTER

19

---

*F*UCK.

Travis stood next to Skeeter, quietly, steadily, listening to Dylan, listening to every fucking word that came out of his boss's mouth, and with every one, he felt his heart harden.

She'd done this to him.

"We don't know that Royce is in Denver because of her. We haven't heard from Rydell yet," Dylan said. "But if she's baited a trap and kills him, we've got a major problem."

She'd baited the trap all right. Travis knew it in his heart. It was all she'd been doing for two goddamn years, playing him for a fool, and trolling the underworld for the man who had destroyed her.

The call he'd gotten hadn't come from Steele

Street. It hadn't come from Skeeter or Dylan.
Gillian had done it. She'd gotten him out of her
way, cut him loose, and he was bleeding all right,
deep, where it hurt.

She should have known better. *Goddamn her.*
She should have known better.

"Hawkins is headed out to Denver International,"
Dylan continued. "Loretta has a team in place to tag
Royce and his boys as they get off their flight from
Las Vegas. Superman will pick them up from there
and follow them in."

"How many men are with Royce?" He needed
to know.

"Five, so it's a full party of six."

Six.

Travis nodded.

That was more than enough to send the night
straight to hell.

"The DEA has confirmed that Royce has
opened a new base of operations in El Salvador,
and that's where Red Dog flew in from today."

"Yes."

"I won't let her turn this town into a bloodbath
tonight," Hart said, and Travis didn't doubt him for
a second. "None of us will survive the repercussions of her killing six people in cold blood without
orders. It doesn't matter that he's the scum of the
earth; somebody with more pull than Grant wants

Royce alive, and I can't have her going through his men like matchsticks until she gets him. We don't make the rules, we follow them, or we've got nothing here."

And nobody doubted that Red Dog could kill Royce and however many of his men she needed to until she got what she wanted, not when she'd had time to set an ambush. Killing people is what she did. Walking the line is what they all did. Crossing it was unacceptable.

He saw Dylan's gaze shift to Skeeter for a heartbeat—and he understood.

Leavenworth. That was the threat hanging over Dylan's head. SDF was the only thing that stood between him and his enemies, not the bad guys out on the world stage, but the ones in Washington, D.C. He had a past that wouldn't hold up under too much scrutiny; a long-ago deal in Moscow, especially, could and would be used against him if the powers-that-be decided they needed to clean up a mess and find a scapegoat. He could go to prison for treason, or he could run, but there was no middle ground for him. There never had been, not from the inception of Special Defense Force, when someone high up at the State Department had saved him from the CIA and a prison cell and given him to General Grant.

Hart would just take his millions and run, and

Skeeter would be with him every step of the way. Skeeter would never do what Gillian had done. Betrayal wasn't part of her, any part of her.

"Call Superman," Travis said, turning to her. He knew what he had to do. "Tell him I'm headed back to Commerce City."

"Maybe," Dylan said, the one word simple, direct, and loaded with enough freight to stop him in his tracks.

Travis turned back to Dylan and met his gaze straight on. He knew what was coming, and it pissed him off.

"If you go back out on the streets tonight, it's going to be as my agent, not as her boyfriend." The words were cold, the orders clear, the threat guaranteed.

Travis didn't say a word at first, because the only two he had were "fuck you." It took every goddamn thing he had and a good thirty seconds before he could come up with, "Yes, sir."

At Dylan's nod, he turned and headed for the stairs. The Steele Street armory was one floor above them, and he needed to gear up before he went hunting for Red Dog. If she ended up with half of the goddamn Damn Dirty Dozen on her tail, it was going to be a bloody night no matter what Dylan wanted or didn't want. Nobody was going to get out of this unscathed.

Goddamn her.

He took the stairs two at a time, because there was no time, not now, not tonight. It had taken him half an hour to get to Steele Street from the Commerce City garage. Dylan had spent the next fifteen minutes reading him the fucking riot act, and it was going to take him at least that to get back to her apartment—if he took the interstate and burned the tires off something a helluva lot faster than his Jeep.

He heard Skeeter come up behind him.

"I'm going to need a car," he said, grabbing his assault vest out of his locker. It was already loaded with everything he needed for a night on the town, including flash bangs and magazines for both his Glock 21 and his HK UMP45 subgun. The only other thing he needed was—exactly what Skeeter handed him out of her locker: a tactical shotgun loaded with double-ought buck. While he was shrugging into his vest, she shoved a handful of breaching loads into one of his pouches.

Nothing was getting between him and Red Dog tonight. Wherever she was, he was going to find her. Wherever she was, he was going to get to her— so help him God and a breaching 12-gauge.

"About that car?" he asked, and Skeeter handed him a key.

"Adeline."

He knew Adeline, Quinn's black, 1968 Yenko Super Camaro. She had a white bumblebee racing stripe hugging her grille and 427 cubic inches of pure rat under her hood putting out 450 horses. She was classic, one of a kind, and off-limits.

"Quinn is going to have your ass, when he finds out you gave me this key."

"He'll have to catch me first," the punk baby rocker girl said.

And with Dylan Hart standing between her and the rest of the world, that was unfuckinglikely.

He'd been standing there for Gillian, for Red Dog, for all the goddamn good that had done him. *Shit*.

Three minutes later, he was running Adeline up through her gears, the beast in her doing what he needed her to do. He hit the ramp onto I-25 and gunned her up to ninety. By the time he slid through the infamous highway intersection at I-25 and I-70 called the Mousetrap, he'd broken a hundred, and Adeline was hitting her stride.

"CAN you locate her, Skeeter?" Dylan would take her down himself, if she'd gone so far over the edge that she was operating outside of the law and killing people while she was on his shift.

"I've been working on it, and I think I've come

up with something that might help us find her. Her phone is basically a standard civilian PDA with a few refinements," Skeeter said, regarding her computer screen. "But she's probably disabled her GPS locator chip."

"If she hasn't, she doesn't have any business working for us," he said.

"Right," Skeeter agreed, tapping a sequence into her keyboard. "I've been hacking deep to see if I can use her provider's law enforcement override and trick her phone into making an emergency call, and I think I've got it working. I'll terminate the call at my computer, and her PDA should keep transmitting her coordinates until the battery dies, or until she tries to use it."

"Or until she gets rid of it," Dylan said. "That's quite a few 'ifs.' "

"It's what we've got," she said, continuing to work her keyboard.

Several more keystroke sequences later, her screen displayed a flashing red triangle superimposed on a large-scale map of Commerce City.

"Okay, I've got it. I'm showing a signal on top of a three-story building close to the SDF garage," she said.

Goddamn it all to hell.

That was it.

"She didn't get very far from home," Dylan said, tight-jawed, looking over his wife's shoulder.

"And she picked a helluva IFP. The girl has the high ground."

No shit.

"And she's got a sniper rifle in her arsenal," he said.

"She won't need the SR-25 for such short range."

Skeeter was right, but somehow, Dylan didn't take much comfort in the fact. There was only one reason for Gillian to be on the rooftops of Commerce City: She was expecting company.

Whatever she'd been doing in El Salvador, she'd made damn sure Tony Royce would come for her.

"Call Superman. Warn him she's up on that building, probably with her crosshairs on her own goddamn door."

"And Travis?"

"Yes." The Angel Boy needed to know his sweetheart had crossed the line. "Can you text her?" If she wasn't answering her goddamn phone, maybe she'd at least read a message.

"Sure," Skeeter said. "But if I do, she'll get an audio cue and maybe toss the damn phone down a drainpipe. Then we really won't be able to track her."

"Key this in, then, but don't transmit it until I say so," Dylan said, printing rapidly on his notepad.

Skeeter looked at the brief message, nodded, then started entering it into her computer.

"*Blade Runner*, her favorite movie," she said. "The director's cut. It's not like you to get sentimental."

"She's got six guys out there who want to kill her, and two who don't want to, but...*shit*." More than anyone at Steele Street, Dylan knew what she'd gone through, but he couldn't allow her actions to stand. She either called herself off, or he was going to do it for her.

Skeeter typed, and Dylan read the message as it showed up on the screen: ROYCE PLUS 5 IN DENVER. BUT REMEMBER, IF YOU'RE NOT COP, YOU'RE LITTLE PEOPLE. CALL ME. LET ME HELP. DYLAN.

CHAPTER

20

MEN: SHOULD WE, or Shouldn't We? Vegetative Deities of the Male Pantheon"—okay, Smith was going to skip that chapter, the same way he'd skipped "Sacred Blood: What It Means to You— Transformative Powers of Menstruation."

Chapter Four, "Postorgasmic Mindstate: Getting There Is Half the Fun—Enlightenment Through Bliss," looked promising, but he wasn't putting a nickel on finding any shameless sorority-girl sex games in it.

He closed the book and turned it over in his hand, looking at the cover one more time. Talk about a marketing scam. This thing had probably been thrown against the wall in every fraternity house in America.

He had figured out why there wasn't a ring on her finger, though—Chapter Six. "Marriage: Why and Why Not? Sanctioned Oppression in Patriarchal Societies."

He'd been married once, briefly, very briefly, apparently just long enough to oppress the woman he'd loved before she'd thrown him out on his ass.

"So what do you think?" she asked, bending over her foot where they were sitting on the bed with their backs propped against the wall with pillows. His Sig was cocked, locked, and loaded. There had been some gunfire coming from the Palacio's courtyard earlier, and he was ready to rock and roll if the party started to move to the third floor. She, on the other hand, had a tiny brush in her fingers and was ready to dab a little polish on one of her toes.

Apparently, at some point during the evening, she'd chipped a nail.

He hadn't noticed, and for the love of God and everything sacred and feminine in the Universe, he didn't know how in the hell she had, either. With all the shit that had hit the fan since he'd seen her out in front of the Hotel Palacio, how in the mother-loving hell had she noticed a chip in the polish on her toenail?

It was the biggest goddamn mystery of the whole friggin' night as far as he was concerned.

Sanctioned oppression—God, that ate at him.

"It's good. Really good," he said. "Inspiring, actually. I'm thinking of writing a book of my own now."

"You are?" She looked up with a warm smile, which almost instantly turned wary. Smart girl. "What kind of book?"

"I haven't thought of a title yet, but I've got the first chapter heading—'Women: Should We or Shouldn't We? And How Many Should We, Before We Don't Anymore?' "

"Jerk."

Whatever.

"Did anybody ever write you and demand their money back?"

Her silence was answer enough.

"So what do you do? Send them a money order?"

"I don't think you actually read the text."

"Well, I'm going to, right after I finish writing my own chapter on marriage."

"Go ahead and tell me," she said with a long-suffering sigh, dabbing an extra bit of lacquer on her baby toe, which as far as he could see had already been adequately covered with candy-apple red polish, the whole freaking square quarter inch of it. "I can tell you've got something you're just dying to get out."

"'Marriage,'" he said. "'Collusion or Delusion?'"

She put the brush back in the bottle and looked up again. "Rough divorce?"

How incredibly insightful.

"She took my socks. My *socks*." He still didn't understand that part. "I came back from Panama to an empty house and an empty sock drawer. So you tell me who was oppressed."

"How long ago did this happen?"

A legitimate question, but he kind of hated how calm she was about it. He was still pissed about his divorce.

"Sixteen months and two girlfriends ago."

"Whirlwind courtship?"

"A hurricane."

"Read Chapter Seven, 'Hormones and Phero-mones: Love or Lust? Emotional and Biological Responses to Sexual Stimuli,' and every place it says 'woman,' put the word 'man,' and every place it says 'man,' put the word 'woman.'"

"Men and women are not interchangeable."

"Oh, pul-lease," she said, rolling her eyes at him.

Oh, pul-lease. God, what gall.

Even worse, now that they were both on the bed, and it would be most helpful for her to be looking her sex-kittenish best, she was coming damn close to actually looking like a feminist. She was wearing his clothes, for crying out loud, men's clothes, and they were sagging, and bagging, and practically falling off, but not nearly falling off enough to suit him.

Biological Responses. He knew a little about biological responses. He was suffering through a biological response, and it wasn't doing anything to improve his mood.

Love or Lust?

No contest, it was lust all the way, baby. *Dammit.*

"How hot do you think it is in here?" she asked, dropping the bottle of polish into her tote and rummaging around for God only knew what to play with next—and he didn't know why in the hell it couldn't be him.

Plenty hot.

"We're pushing a hundred, easy." With the broken windows barricaded with the chiffonier, even though there was open space above it, there was damn little breeze getting into the room. The electricity was still out, so the fan wasn't working. They had two candles burning, and by his guess, they were each putting out about a thousand or so calories of added heat with every minute they were lit—and she was sitting on the bed with him.

Hellishly hot.

"And one of us obviously gets a little crabby in the heat," she said, still rummaging.

It wasn't the heat making him crabby. She didn't want to hear about what was making him crabby.

"How's your butt?" It was a legitimate question, he didn't care what anybody said.

"It *hurts*," she said, and stuck her tongue out at him—and he came *that* close to jumping her. Right then. Right there.

If she wanted to stick her tongue out at him, she could at least stick it where it—

"Here you go," she said, handing him a juice box and interrupting his train of thought.

"You've got juice boxes in there?" He hadn't noticed them when all her junk had been piled on the bed. Of course, it had been an amazingly big pile of junk, and there had been all that money jumbled up in all of it.

"And chips. Do you want a bag of chips? Or a granola bar?"

No. He didn't want to eat, he wanted to—

"Chocolate? It's melted, but it's still in its wrapper, so you can lick it off."

Yes. Licking sounded good. Too good. What in the hell was wrong with him?

Not enough danger, he decided. Yes, there were a few explosions here and there, and some semiautomatic weapon fire going off out on the street now and then—but none of it was directed toward them. There were dozens of people staying at the Palacio, and he bet every single one of them was doing what he and Honey were doing: waiting out the night, knowing the Palacio had held up through countless coups, innumerable guerilla and terrorist attacks, and a couple of outright wars.

No doubt, the damn place would still be standing come morning.

"I know why you're angry."

No, she didn't. He never gave anything away, not in word or deed, and she couldn't read his mind.

"I've confused you."

Okay, maybe she had something there.

"You're a guy, and when guys read the title of the book, they expect something light and maybe a little racy," she said.

More than a little racy, he could have told her, and sex was not a subject that guys took lightly, ever.

"And maybe they expect some real 'nuts and bolts'-type material."

Definitely on the nuts and bolts.

"And maybe some photos."

Double definitely on the photos.

"But then they read the chapter headings, and the book starts looking like a feminist manifesto with no nuts and bolts and no photos." After more rummaging, she finally pulled out a small bag of potato chips and a melted candy bar. "But until you read the actual text, you can't have a clear idea of the message I built my thesis on, so if you haven't read it, you don't really know how it all turns out." She carefully opened the candy bar, then tore open the bag of chips.

"How does it turn out?" He watched, slightly fascinated, as she took a chip and scooped a little melted chocolate onto it.

"Well, with what you've read, it wouldn't be out of line for you to think I'm an antiman, anti-heterosexual sex, hard-core, women's studies lesbian."

A shiver of alarm went through him, his first of the night. Guys shooting at him, he could deal with. Guys shooting at each other, he understood. Bombs and riots, no problem. But the thought of Honey York being a lesbian rattled his internal gyroscope.

"I'm not," she assured him, lifting the chocolate-dipped chip to his mouth. "Open up."

He did, and in went the salty, sweet treat with the tips of her fingers brushing against his lips.

Heat, the good kind, instantly grabbed him in the gut and groin.

"I like heterosexual sex," she said, and ridiculously, the heat spread to his brain.

"Good," he said, as if that was an astute comment to the best news he'd had all night. She liked sex with guys. He was glad to hear it. Damn glad.

"I'm not saying it's a cure-all for the world's problems. I know it's just one part of life, but I can't help but believe, and what I put in the book, especially in the concluding chapters, is that if every now and then you can just jump into bed, or up on the kitchen table, or into the back seat of your car with your sweetie-pie and make love until you're completely wrung out and you've both melted into puddles on the floor, that you can face the rest of life's problems a little easier. Don't you agree?"

"Yes," he answered, his gaze riveted on her. His wires were crossed, his blood rushing around inside him in all the best ways—and his answer was an unqualified yes.

"It's more of a sexual partnership philosophy," she said.

Yes. Full-speed ahead on sexual partnership philosophy, and that was another first for him. He couldn't remember ever getting too damn philosophical about sex before. It seemed to negate the whole point of sex, which for him—and he thought he was speaking for quite a few guys with this—was basically not to have to think for a while, about anything, except sex.

"All three locations," he added, just to make things absolutely clear. He was on board for the bed, the table, and the car.

Anything.

Everything.

With her.

Four hours ago, if someone had told him that he'd be completely turned inside out and on by somebody named Honoria York-Lytton who would be feeding him chocolate-covered potato chips while they were sitting on the bed in his dumpy hotel room, he would have said they were certifiable.

Instead, it was him who'd lost his ever-loving mind.

A point that really hit home when her phone rang.

It was a jazzy ring tone, a tune he almost recognized, and it was coming out of her giant tote bag.

A friggin' phone.

Fuck. He groaned. What in the ever-loving hell had he been thinking?

Honest to God, somewhere between when he'd grabbed her on the veranda and when he'd gotten so cozy with her on the mattress, he should have thought to ask her if she had a phone.

Sure, he'd been a little busy with the glass and the gunmen, and with securing the room and trying to keep his brains above his belt, but he still should have thought to ask.

She dug the phone out, a pink phone, of course, and flipped it open. "*Bonjour.*"

And of course with the "bonjour." *Geez.*

"Hey, Mitzi . . . sure, that'll be great . . . okay, then, next Wednesday." She flipped the phone shut, and he stared at it for a couple of long seconds. *Mitzi.*

"Where did Mitzi call you from?" he finally asked. In his experience, there weren't too many women in El Salvador named Mitzi.

"Washington."

"D.C.?"

"*Um-hmmm,*" she said, scooping chocolate on another chip and holding it up to his mouth.

"Can I borrow it?" he asked, then opened up and took the chip, just to feel the brush of her fingertips again. It was a cheap shot, but he loved it. "I have an important call I need to make." That was one way to put it, he guessed, one kind of understated, incredibly stupid, oversimplified way.

"Sure," she said, handing the phone over and fixing him another chip. "Just don't talk long, if that's okay. I'm running a little low on the battery, and Julia will probably check in with me sooner or later since I haven't shown up at the church yet tonight."

And she wasn't going to be showing up at the damn church tonight, period. He'd thrown that damn plan out the minute she'd told him, when she'd first come out of the bathroom. Carting a quarter of a million dollars across San Luis in a fricking tote bag would be fine, if it was him doing the toting. But asking Honey to do it bordered on the insane, something he was going to make very clear to Sister Julia and Father Bartolo in the morning, when he *would* be the one toting and delivering the orphan money. He'd promised her, just to keep her from trying to do it on her own, and maybe just so he could sleep at night for the rest of his life.

Orphan money. *Geezus.* He was supposed to be down here tracking Red Dog, *la cazadora espectral*, and keeping tabs on Tony motherfucking Royce— not saving orphans.

And all he'd needed to do was make one lousy phone call to an annex of the Pentagon to confirm with a general of the United States Army that he'd tracked the general's black ops contractor to the last goddamn place she should have been, and found out that the international criminal who had destroyed her life was not in residence, but that she'd left her address so he could look her up back home in Colorado.

General Grant needed to know it. Christian

Hawkins needed to know it, and like it or not, Dylan Hart needed to know it—and once the information got to Hart, Smith could guarantee that Red Dog was going to wish she'd thought twice about those cans of red spray paint she'd used on Royce's villa.

HONEY was running out of time and ideas. She really didn't think she could put him to sleep with chocolate-covered potato chips and orange juice, but he'd turned down her offer of more liquor, and she didn't have it in her to slip him a Xanax.

She just didn't. *Dammit.*

She hadn't lied to him, not really, but there was a bit more to Julia's story than orphans, and his really sweet offer of taking the money to St. Mary's in the morning wasn't going to work.

She had until three A.M. to get to the church, and not a minute later, or Julia would be gone, and she wouldn't have her money, and Honey would never forgive herself.

C. Smith Rydell pushed off the bed and took her phone with him into the bathroom, but unlike her, when she'd secretly made her last three phone calls under the pretext of potty breaks, he didn't close the door.

She was thinking he might have the instincts of

a Rottweiler, or a bullmastiff, some kind of highly bred guard dog. Honestly, she didn't know what would make him think he needed to keep an eye on her, or why in the world he would care what she did—but he was watching her like a hawk, like she might make a dash for it.

Which was exactly what she was trying to figure out how to do—to make a dash out the door, down the street, and into the god-awful fray to save the sister she loved.

Sometimes Honey hated her mother, and never more so than when Julia Ann-Marie was in trouble up to her neck and sinking fast. Maternal neglect had been the problem from the get-go. There were three brothers between her and Julia, but Honey didn't remember ever paying the boys too much mind. They'd all gotten plenty of attention. They were the York-Lyttons who would make sure the world didn't run out of York-Lyttons for at least another generation—God forbid. Sometimes Honey wasn't sure the world was noticing nearly as much as her father thought or was hoping.

But then one day, something new had come into the York household, the softest, tiniest, pinkest bundle of baby Honey had ever seen, and everything in her ten-year-old heart had instantly fallen in love.

Julia had been hers from the first tiny spoonful

of cereal Honey had put in her mouth, until Honey
had pulled her out of that blood-splattered elevator in the Hotel Langston on the island of Malanca
off the coast of Honduras two years ago. Julia's
husband had been crumpled in the corner, his
body torn apart by the same kind of gunfire Honey
could hear out on the street in San Luis.

That was the day Honey had lost her.

She was getting ready to lose her all over again,
and there wasn't a damn thing she could do about
it. Talk about a goddamn hard lesson to learn.

Julia had chosen a path Honey could barely
comprehend, but she could ease her way. A quarter
of a million dollars in small bills went a helluva
long way in Central America, whether a person
was fixing orphanages or supporting the families of
farmers displaced by a consortium of coffee corpo-
rations, the church's newest rallying point against a
government trying to usurp its power.

Honey was all for helping people. It was Julia's
hands-on approach to saving the sick, feeding the
hungry, and easing other people's suffering
through prayer and judicious infusions of cash that
made her lose sleep at night, because it could take
a frightful toll.

It had taken a frightful toll.

Politics was a deadly game, especially in the
Third World, the world Julia's young doctor hus-

band had meddled in too deeply, trying to change things that couldn't be changed, trying to improve the lot of people whose lot in life couldn't be improved. Dr. Carl Bakkert had made Honey look like a realist, and that was a tragic statement on the frightful depths of idealism some people could sink to and still not be prepared for the consequences.

So here she was, running out of time and short on ideas, and wondering why, with all the huge problems she was dealing with, one of the biggest seemed to be that Smith was cute.

Really cute, in a bigger, badder, faster, stronger, smarter sort of way that she could guarantee caught a lot of women's attention. It had caught hers from the moment she'd seen him sitting in front of the cantina. Sure, he'd looked like a thousand other slackers she'd seen in dozens of other tropical beach towns all over the world, but not quite—not with that body, and not with the calmly cold expression he'd had on his face. As relaxed as he'd been, he'd looked like a man on a mission.

She shouldn't have been surprised he'd been the one to reach her first when she'd been running from all those men. Everything about C. Smith Rydell said he was used to winning, to getting what he wanted—and he wanted her.

She knew it, which just made the whole "cute"

problem that much worse. She was only in El Salvador for one reason, and it was not to find herself attracted to some mysterious guy in serious need of a haircut—no matter how cute he was, no matter how thick and dark his eyelashes were, no matter that every time she looked at his mouth, all she could think was . . . trouble.

But he'd saved her almost before she'd even known she needed saving, thinking way ahead of the game, being kind of romantically heroic, yelling at those guys through the door, ready to take it all to the next level. Whatever it took.

And he had that whole "I'm in charge—get used to it" attitude that normally would have had her explaining a few of the realities of life to him— except he was the biggest wall of reality she'd ever run into. She didn't understand it. She just knew it, and it was a comfort, to wash up against that much solid confidence and know it wasn't going to let her down, at least not in a hotel room in San Luis in the middle of a riot.

And then there was the heat.

God, the heat.

Every time he sat down next to her, it was all she could do not to squirm—but she wouldn't. Honoria York-Lytton did not squirm, especially in front of men, and most especially not in front of strange men. And yet it was wonderful. And it was awful. It was the kind of heat that got girls in trouble—and it was happening with him.

She needed to get a grip. Heat and Smith were not her problems. Her problem was that she was going out the door and into the street, one way or the other, and in her heart she knew that even with the map she had in her tote, and even if she managed to get her gun and her bullet back, it was going to be damn hard getting to the church.

Damn hard.

Dangerous.

Rain in the mountains had washed out the road Julia and Father Bartolo had been taking from the rebel camp, so they were running as late as Honey, and every hour later that it got was one less hour Honey would have with Julia before she disappeared again, for God knew how long. It had been eight months, two weeks, and five days since the last time Honey had seen her, and the thought of going that long again broke her heart right down to the center of her soul.

Julia was hers.

She did not want to be late, and it was two miles to St. Mary's from the Royal Suites Hotel. The Hotel Palacio was only a couple of blocks closer. With detours to take into account, she wanted an hour to get there. She wanted to be waiting when Julia showed up.

So here she was, in a hotel room on a sweltering summer night in a tropical country coming apart at the seams, with only a couple of hours before she threw herself into the breach and committed a crime that would probably get her shot by the local government, if she didn't manage that all by herself getting to St. Mary's.

And there was C. Smith Rydell, the Rock of Gibraltar with a pair of Ray-Bans tucked into his T-shirt pocket, pacing the bathroom floor and making her hot all over.

CHAPTER

21

THIS IS ONE of those parties where you wish you'd brought your own booze, your own music, and your own rules of engagement," Hawkins said, holding his phone in one hand and a pair of binoculars in the other.

"Don't start with me," Dylan said.

"Sorry, boss, but I'm looking at more trouble in one place than I've seen in a while." He was lying on the roof of the nondescript Buick he'd taken out of the Steele Street garage, watching four of Royce's men pull gear out of the black Expedition they'd rented at the airport. "They've definitely got the girl's number. They're three blocks west of the garage, parked in the old Geiss Fastener lot, and it looks like they're loading up to go in on foot. From the looks of the gun cases they're pulling out of the back of their SUV, I'd say they're getting ready to seriously break some laws."

"I'm sure they are, but let's keep Loretta out of it as long as possible, preferably all night long. Have you gotten a positive ID on Royce?" Dylan asked.

"No," Hawkins said. "Loretta's men said he got in the SUV, and there haven't been any stops since I picked them up."

"If they're going in on foot, they must figure she's waiting for them."

"*Absolutamente,* boss. They're going hunting. Otherwise, why not just drive up and go knock on the door."

"I wonder—what in the hell did Gillian do in El Salvador?"

"So Rydell is still off the radar?"

"Somebody needs to teach that boy how to use a phone."

"Well, whatever it was she did, it sure got the job done," he said. "We need to send Frankie T a nice thank-you note, or we would have been left out in the cold—*geezus.*"

"What?"

"Here's an ID for you. Zane Lowe just got out of the Expedition. That bastard has to be fair game anywhere in the United States. Have Skeeter see what she can find on him. Hell, I could probably make money taking him out."

"Let's just pick Gillian up and get her under wraps. When these boys come up empty-handed, they'll leave."

"Bull. Now that they've tracked her down, they'll be back. We should move on them and talk fast later."

"Not tonight, Superman. Not when the Feds are watching."

He swore, one succinct word, but Dylan was right, for tonight.

"Yeah. I guess we better drop a little thank-you to Setineri, too. I take it Red Dog hasn't answered her phone, either?"

"No. But she's holding steady on the warehouse roof."

"She'll move fast once she gets a load of these boys. How far is Travis from the garage?"

"Five minutes out. He's driving Adeline."

"That's a helluva sound signature. She'll hear Addy's pipes whether she's paying attention to her phone or not."

"It's why Skeeter gave the Angel Boy Quinn's newest piece of iron," Dylan said. There wasn't a person at Steele Street who wouldn't recognize the sound of one of Quinn's Camaros. "Gillian will know somebody is coming in to get her, and maybe that will make her think twice before she does something we'll all regret."

"Maybe," Hawkins said.

"Or maybe not," Dylan said.

Yeah, that's what Hawkins thought, too. He'd trained her, done his best to put her back together, but there were parts of that girl nobody was ever going to reach.

Geezus. He looked up from his binoculars for a second, scanning the streets around him. Colorado weather had just kicked in big-time, the temperature dropping a good ten degrees in less than that many seconds. The wind was coming down the alley to his north, blowing trash and taking the heat out of the air, and replacing it with something they hadn't had in weeks—rain, a soft, steady sheet of it.

And the weathermen strike out again, he thought in disgust. Nobody had predicted rain.

"Get your headset on," Dylan continued. "Skeeter is going to connect you to Travis. It'll be radio communications from here on out, and Superman?"

"Yeah?"

"If you get turned around down there in the alleys and lose these guys, be sure and let us know."

"Fuck you."

"Yeah. You, too. Good hunting."

FROM THE PRIVACY of the bathroom, Smith brought up the menu on Honey's pink flip phone and wrote down its number. Then he keyed in a different, thirteen-digit number, verified it onscreen, and hit "send."

He got an answer on the second ring.

"Drug Enforcement Agency," an official-sounding female voice said.

Damn. Just his luck. He'd been hoping someone else would be answering that number tonight—anyone else.

"Carol? It's Smith Rydell," he said, stopping his pacing and sitting on the edge of the bathtub, where he could keep an eye on Honey in the other room.

"So?" the woman said, her voice turning glacial.

She'd always been quick, just not quick enough not to get wrapped up in the rebound of his divorce.

"I need a favor," he said.

"You don't work here anymore, remember?"

"I'm in trouble."

"Then get yourself out."

He could almost see her handset heading back toward its cradle.

"Carol, Carol," he said quickly, and loudly, in case she really had already moved to hang up on him.

"Go on."

"I've got a problem. I'm in El Salvador on a civilian cell phone, and I need to call my commanding officer on a secure channel. The situation here is somewhere between urgent and desperate. Can you help me?"

"Are you trying to get me fired, Smith? Call the embassy," she said curtly.

The instant he'd heard her voice, he'd known this wouldn't be easy. It had been a rough breakup, and it had been him doing all the breaking.

"That's part of my problem," he said, rising from the edge of the tub and pacing over to the window. "I need to do this without State or anyone else knowing about it for a while. Carol, please."

"You are trying to get me fired, you jerk."

"I am a jerk, you're right." And he'd never been more of a jerk than after his divorce. "But I've got reason to believe one of my teammates is in danger, and if I can make the call, maybe I can keep her from getting hurt."

"*Her?*" The tone of voice was unmistakable, pure bitch.

Ouch. He hadn't known Carol still cared quite so much.

"An operator who goes by the name Red Dog."

There was a moment's silence, then, "*La cazadora espectral?* You're working with Red Dog? *The* Red Dog?"

Well, that set him back a bit, and yes, as far as he knew, he was working with *the* Red Dog. He was pretty sure there was only one—thank God.

"Yes."

"Wow. Tell her nice hits in Colón."

Geezus, news traveled fast.

"They were, and I did." He looked out the window, checking the street. The situation hadn't changed. It was still chaos with subguns and tire fires.

"*Oh, my, God.*" Carol practically swooned over the phone. "You were there? With her? In Colón?"

Normally, that was a question he wouldn't have answered, but he was in trouble, and he did need help, and something was telling him he'd just stumbled onto a way to get it.

"Yes," he said, counting on being able to work this whole Red Dog thing to his advantage, and hers.

"Is she as amazing as they say?"

"Yes." An amazing amount of trouble.

"And beautiful?"

"Very." In her own kick-ass, take-no-prisoners, tough-girl way. When Red Dog walked into a room, people noticed, and a good many of them stepped back. It was an interesting phenomenon to observe. She wasn't that big, but she managed to dominate a good bit of the space around herself— space nobody intruded on, not without reason or her permission.

"And is it true that she doesn't remember her own name?"

"Yes." And he guessed that made it official. He was now president of the Red Dog Fan Club. "She knows her name, but only because she's been told. She doesn't remember it." Neither did he remember Carol ever being quite so breathlessly excited about anything, except during sex. This was a new side of her.

"How *awful*," she said in a way that sounded a lot like "how cool," as in "how romantically tragic, to lose your mind and become a vengeful killer."

He didn't want to tell her that there was no vengeance involved. It was Gillian's job, no more, no less, except when it came to Tony Royce, which brought him back to the point of the phone call.

"She's in trouble, Carol, and I'm her only hope." Just call him Obi-Wan.

"Okay," Carol said after a slight hesitation. "But I'm doing this for her, not you; I want to make that perfectly clear."

Got it, he thought.

"I appreciate it, Carol." God, had he really made love to this woman? It never failed to amaze him how much animosity could be generated by intimacy.

"What's your phone number?"

He read it to her, and she read it back for him to verify.

"And who do you want to call?"

"General Buck Grant, in Washington, D.C."

There was another moment of silence, before she spoke.

"You're with *them* now?"

He wasn't answering that question, and after a moment's silence, Carol knew it.

"Okay. Fine. Be that way. Press your 'end' key twice," she said, "and leave your phone turned on. I'm going to set up a satellite link between Grant's office and the U.S. Embassy in San Salvador."

When he and Carol had first met, she'd been assigned to the Central American desk. Now she was a communications supervisor with all the tricks up her sleeve and at her fingertips.

"I'm going to put you on a local channel that will connect your phone to the embassy and simultaneously block your cell tower reception and transmission," she continued. "Give me about five minutes. If it doesn't work, I'll call you back from here."

He did as he'd been told, pressing the "end" key twice, before walking back into the bedroom. He knew what she was trying to do, and he was grateful. If it worked, Grant's transmissions would be uplinked to the DOS secure satellite network, terminated at the San Salvador embassy's computer, and digitally transmitted to his phone at minimum power. His transmissions would follow the same route in reverse. The only opportunity for anyone to monitor the conversation would be if they could intercept the 0.6-watt transmissions between Honey's cell phone and the embassy computer.

The risk was considered acceptable in an emergency situation, and the route bought him the hours he needed. The embassy computer logs wouldn't be reviewed until after the morning office staff arrived at work, between nine and ten o'clock. By then, he'd be on a plane headed back to the States.

Stretching out on the bed, he settled in to wait. Five minutes.

His gaze strayed to Honey sitting next to him.

A lot could happen in five minutes, but he doubted if anything would.

She was busy taking all the bows and bobby pins out of her hair and putting them in a zebra-striped, zippered makeup bag trimmed in red leather. There was a reason she had so many pins, the same reason she'd had her hair pulled into a French twist. Unleashed, it was wild, out of control, going crazy with the heat and the humidity.

"Nice hairdo," he said, just to get her to stick her tongue out at him again.

She didn't disappoint, and he had a feeling that's why she'd done it for the second freaking time. She knew he liked it.

She knew he wanted to kiss her.

She knew every man she met wanted to kiss her.

Women, especially hot, spoiled, beautiful women, were enough to turn a guy into an absolute idiot, and he was disappointed as hell to find out he was no exception, not when it came to her.

Geezus. He usually had more sense.

Finished with the last pin, she ran her hands up

into her hair and slipped her fingers through the whole tawny blond mess, stirring it up, rubbing her scalp, giving it all a little shake.

He wanted to look away. Honestly, he did, but he couldn't.

When she was done, she gave her hair a final toss over her shoulder and met his gaze, very directly, across the very short length of bed separating them.

Very short.

"Interesting phone call, Smith," she said.

"You couldn't have heard my phone call all the way from over here."

The look she gave him said only one thing: *Oh, yeah?*

Shit.

He hadn't said anything too incriminating or classified, but he hated to think he'd misjudged the distance between them, or the acuity of a sorority girl's hearing.

"What do you think you heard?"

"I heard you admit to a woman named Carol that you're a jerk, which tells me *something* must have been going on between the two of you."

Okay, she'd heard plenty, probably everything.

"Not as much as you're thinking," he assured her.

"So it was just sex?"

Geezus.

"It was none of your business."

"I think it's cool that you know you're a jerk. Most guys aren't that aware of their shortcomings," she said, digging back into her tote bag.

He grinned. She was such a piece of work.

"I'm not most guys," he said, which got him another roll of her eyes.

His grin broadened.

"What about the other woman you mentioned? Red Dog? The one who doesn't know her own name? What's her story?"

He held her gaze but didn't say anything.

"That's a pretty interesting name, Red Dog," she said, undaunted.

"You might want to forget you ever heard it."

"Betcha I don't."

"Betcha you should."

"You don't scare me anymore."

He could, in about half a second flat. He'd actually had quite a bit of training in how to scare the holy fucking crap out of anybody in less than half a second flat. It was considered a basic skill in his line of work. A guy had to have it, or he couldn't do the job.

But Honey wasn't a job. She was an accident, a wondrous, fluffy-haired, green-eyed, barefoot accident with soft pink shimmery lips.

"What happened to your red lipstick?"

"Makeup remover," she said, showing him a small, wadded-up tissue with candy-apple-red smears on it. "I changed my outfit, so I changed my lipstick."

Well, well, well, who would ever have believed it? His green parrot shirt and khaki cargoes had been elevated to the status of "outfit."

He honestly hadn't thought he owned any "outfits." But he could see it. Sure. She'd rolled up the pants legs, which gave the trousers a certain *esprit de* something or another. She'd tied the tails of the shirt, to better accent her waist, which was something he had never, ever, *ever* done with his green parrot shirt. Or the blue one. Or with any shirt he owned.

She wasn't wearing a bra with the shirt, which he never did either, but somehow, the whole braless thing looked really enticing on her, whereas he'd bet his ass nobody had ever noticed it on him.

And then there were the buttons. He was a casual kind of guy, but that last button she'd left unbuttoned? He usually kept it buttoned. It was button number three. Nonetheless, he was awfully glad that she'd left it undone. It was just enough to tease him, without pushing him straight over the edge.

"You smell good." Really good. Not that she

hadn't smelled good before, but now she smelled good in a different, really riveting way.

"Thank you. It's Paradise," she said, lifting a tiny bottle out of her makeup bag to show him.

It was very pretty, all blue and pink and green, with the glass all swirly.

"If you like, we could spritz a little under your shirt. It'll sort of warm up on your chest and be very comforting."

Yes, he could see how that might work, maybe— but maybe not. For the sure shot, he needed to be the one doing the spritzing, as in spritzing a little more under her shirt, warming himself up on her chest, and just letting the whole night sink into the paradise of having his face buried between the soft mounds of her bodacious—

Geezus! The phone rang in his hand and damn near gave him a heart attack.

He snapped it open, felt like a fool, and said, "Rydell."

"*Buenas noches, pendejo,*" Grant growled. "I understand you're in El Salvador. Care to fill me in?"

CHAPTER

23

GILLIAN HEARD Adeline long before she saw the rat-powered Camaro pull up in the alley bordering the Commerce City garage. Nobody tuned headers like Quinn. Nobody did it better.

Damn. She wiped the rain off her face and rose to her feet. The last thing she needed was for one of the SDF operators to show up at the garage tonight.

But she was in more trouble than that, way more trouble. It wasn't Quinn Younger who got out of the classic piece of muscle.

It was Travis, and he was definitely in Vengeful Angel mode, packing enough firepower to do some real damage—and he knew exactly where she was hiding in the shadows.

He came around the back of the Camaro, slinging a shotgun across his front, carrying a subgun, and raking the warehouse's rooftop with his gaze. At the end of the alley, he stopped, and she saw him say something into the headset he was wearing.

With a steadiness that unnerved her all the way down to the middle of her gut, he brought his gaze back across the rooftop and stopped dead on her. She saw his mouth move again, saw his short nod, and then he sent her a message, loud and clear. He raised his arm and pointed his finger straight at her: *Stay put, baby. I'm coming for you.*

She was frozen in place for all of two god-awful seconds, frozen by the fear of what she'd done, cutting him out of her private mission.

Then her brain kicked back in.

The hell he was, she thought, and the hell she would. This wasn't his fight, and she wasn't staying put anywhere.

She holstered her Contender back inside her vest and pulled a coil of 7mm climbing rope out of a pocket. Dropping low onto the roof, she peered over the short wall to the street below—and he'd already disappeared.

Goddamn. They'd played this game too many times, war-gamed this game too many times, for him to be anything except damn near unstoppable. The key was in the "damn near."

If he was coming up, she was going down. The best anchor points for her rope were on the other side of the building, but if she was quick, damn quick, she thought one of the cutouts in the wall would hold long enough for her to double her rope through it and slide down three stories to the street. She could retrieve the rope by pulling on one of the free ends.

She had one of her fast-rope gloves on and was getting ready to slip into the other one, when her phone signaled her that she had a text message.

Holy freaking crap.

But suddenly, she knew how Travis had known exactly where to find her—somebody at Steele Street had hacked her phone, and it had to be Baby Bang. She pulled the phone out of her back pocket, swearing under her breath as she flipped it open.

Then she grinned.

ROYCE PLUS 5 IN DENVER.

It was about fucking time.

The grin widened, lifting the corner of her lips, but it didn't last long.

Angel was here, and that was no good.

She scanned the area. The dry creek bed where they played paintball with Johnny Ramos like their lives depended on it would be a good place to take him. Junked cars, piles of old tires, a couple of broken Dumpsters—the place was full of stuff to hide behind and fences to keep people in, or at least slow them down. She could take him into Sand Creek and slip back out without him knowing. By the time he figured out he was in the creek bed alone, she'd be long gone.

Her gaze went back to the text message on her phone.

ROYCE PLUS 5 IN DENVER. BUT REMEMBER, IF YOU'RE NOT COP, YOU'RE LITTLE PEOPLE. CALL ME. LET ME HELP. DYLAN.

Blade Runner. She'd watched it dozens of times. Poor Zhora, the Nexus 6 hit girl, that's what she felt like sometimes, an enhanced android trained to kill, something not quite right. But she wasn't going down like Zhora. It wasn't going to be a blade runner or one of Royce's men who got her. Her demise, when it came, would come from inside herself. XT7 had taken the first thirty-three years of her life, and she was afraid it was going to take the last two—the two she'd spent with Angel.

But five guys, hell, that was a lot of men, especially given the kind of men Royce hired. One at a time had been her plan from the beginning, for them to not have a clue where she was and how she was killing them off, and then, once she got the information out of the one she left alive, she'd go for Royce.

And when he was gone, she'd be done. The rest of her life could play out as best it could, what was left of it, which didn't feel like very damn much—not tonight, it didn't.

The faintest trickle of sensation slipped up her arm from the inside, and she swore again. *Bullshit.* This was not going to happen, not now.

She shook out her hand, keeping her fingers spread. Sometimes that helped, if the problem started slow enough, was light enough, and she hoped to hell tonight was one of those times. She'd already had one episode. That usually worked it out of her for a while. She shook her hand twice, then squeezed it into a fist, closing the fingers tight, and she breathed. It wasn't much, but it was all she had until Dr. Brandt came up with something better, something she could shoot herself up with to negate the symptoms of having a whole boatload of crap jacked into her system and just having to live with it.

Opening her hand, she jerked on her other glove, then slipped her rope through the cutout and dropped over the side of the building. Halfway down, she heard the blast of a breaching load coming out of a 12-gauge somewhere on the other side of the building. *Fuck.* They'd never blown the freaking door off the warehouse before.

Blast or no blast, though, she didn't stop for a second, just kept sliding, using her feet to hold the rope steady.

When she hit the street, she looked up and started pulling the rope down, one long, slinky jerk at a time. Glancing east, she saw nothing, and by the time she looked west, it was too late.

He was there, coming out of the darkness and the rain, and when he grabbed her arm, she knew her time was up. He hadn't gone into the building and headed for the stairs. He'd faked her out.

"Game over, babe," he growled. His hair was plastered to his face, his expression one she'd never seen on him before: fury, and it struck her deep in her core. "The next time I tie you up, I'm leaving you there." His voice was low, hard, and it scared her almost as much as the look on his face.

"That's mean."

"And this *isn't?*" He gave her a small, short shake.

She could tell he wanted to shake her harder, to say more, wanted to say things he might regret. It was in the tightness of the hold he had on her arm. It was in the way he'd dragged her close and almost had her up on her toes. He wanted to break something, and all signs were pointing to her.

She wouldn't let him. He had to know that. She'd only let him have so much of his anger at her, and then she'd have to shut him down, if she could.

And if she couldn't, it was going to be over between them, and wasn't that the price she'd been willing to pay? To lose him forever so she could have her vengeance?

God, it had never seemed simple, but faced with the reality of his face, with his coldness, and the fierce grip he had on her arm, she had to wonder what in the fuck she'd been thinking she was going to get away with.

Nothing.

Not like this.

He had never hurt her, not once, not in thought, word, or deed, not in two years, but he was coming damn close to hurting her now.

He'd never marked her, not once, not ever, but he was leaving marks on her now. She could feel the strength of his fingers digging into her arm, the bruises that would be there in the morning.

"I've got her," he said, and she knew he wasn't talking to her, but into his headset. "Rog—*fuck! Move.*"

A bullet cracked by their heads.

He threw her behind him and took a knee on

the asphalt, his UMP45 spitting a short burst into the night.

Fuck, move was a helluva command—for some other girl.

She got out of his way and backed him up, drawing her night-scoped TC with lightning speed and firing a .223 round into the target she had almost instantly acquired—if it moved, she saw it—and whoever "it" had been, they weren't anymore. She saw the figure crumple to the street, and she and Angel were both moving, fast, fast, fast, along the side of the building, to cover.

CHAPTER

24

SHE WAS IN the bathroom.

Singing.

Smith could hear her through the closed door, singing some song he'd heard on the radio and doing a damn good job of it.

The night was wearing thin.

He'd lain in hides with Red Dog or Kid for hours on end, sometimes days, and been more relaxed than he was lying in bed in the Hotel Palacio with Honey York singing in the bathroom.

He thought he might be falling in love. That was the problem. He was prone to it, spur-of-the-moment lust turning his brains to mush. Sometimes sex took care of the problem, and sometimes sex only made it worse. He had a feeling that, with

Honey, sex would only make it worse. She was so . . . unexpected. He didn't have a category for Harvard-educated, trust-fund, sex-kitten feminists. She was just a little hard for him to wrap his mind around.

He didn't think he'd have any trouble getting anything else wrapped around her. His mind, truly, was the only sticking point, and since he was well on the way to losing it, there might be hope for the night after all.

Or not, he thought, when another explosion rocked the hotel from about a block over.

Geezus. Fuck.

He swore and brushed at the plaster drifting down from the ceiling, and would have gotten it all off himself if she hadn't jerked the bathroom door open, wild-eyed.

"That . . . that was big, and close," she said breathlessly, her hand white-knuckled on the doorknob.

Yes, it had been close—

Another explosion rocked the room from just outside on the goddamn street.

—but not as close as that one.

And what in the holy hell was her shirt doing unbuttoned? Completely unbuttoned?

What had she been doing in the bathroom? Singing with her shirt unbuttoned?

Who did that?

And why?

There was only one answer, and it made his head spin: shameless sorority girl self-help sex games. And just as he was getting ready to get himself all worked up over that, he noticed the washcloth in her other hand, dripping water down the doorjamb.

Okay. Take a breath, Smith, old boy. There was nothing shameless about trying to cool off in a hotel room that had broken the hundred-and-five-degree barrier a good hour back.

He pushed himself off the bed and went to look over the top of the chiffonier. Another explosion like that last one, and he might have to reconsider staying in the Palacio.

He looked into the street and felt his gut churn. *Shit.* Then somebody else, a woman, noticed the guy who'd been blown to pieces, and a scream rent the air—and he meant rent, like a hundred-and-twenty-decibel *schism* of sound tearing through the night. It was bloodcurdling, a sound of utter, senseless shock, and the kind of uncomprehending disbelief that broke people's minds.

Fuck. He ran his hand over his chest, an instinctive gesture. Yeah, his heart was still beating, and the woman was still screaming, and then he heard it. Another sound. A small sound.

He looked toward the bathroom, and Honey was standing there, her face pale, the washcloth clutched to her chest, the straps on her bow-tied platforms unbuckled and flying out on either side of her ankles—and she was overwhelmed and falling apart, one soft gasping sob at a time.

And that's when he gave in.

He lifted his arm and beckoned to her with his palm up: *Come to me.*

And she did, all but throwing herself across the room and into his arms.

It was sweet, and hot, and a little crazy. She still had her washcloth, and somehow, instead of just wrapping her arms around him, she'd gotten her hands under his T-shirt, all the way under, and water was running down his back and down into his pants, which made her feel like kind of a sloppy mess in his arms.

But he wasn't complaining.

No. He was breathing, slow, and steady, and deep, and holding on to her with his face buried in the silky, tawny cloud of her hair, and he was deciding to do it with her. Right now. In this dumpy hotel room with the night falling apart all around.

So he kissed the top of her head, and breathed her in, and filled himself up with Paradise and Honey, and with her platform shoes on her feet, he didn't have to bend too far down to get his mouth

on her face, on her soft, soft skin, on her cheek...
on her lips.

She opened her mouth under his, but he didn't
kiss her, not yet, because it was a crazy, crazy moment, a place outside of time, with the woman
screaming and the night smelling of burning rub-
ber, and the woman in his arms feeling like so
much more than made sense.

He was a careful guy. He didn't give anything
away, least of all to a woman he didn't know.

"Hi," she said, her mouth barely touching his,
her breath so soft against his lips—and despite
everything, he grinned.

Yeah. Hi.

"I'm a little scared," she said. "That woman out
there, she sounds like...like I shouldn't look out
the window."

"No, baby," he said, brushing his lips so softly
across hers. He wasn't letting her anywhere near
the window.

"I think...I think—" She stopped and a tremor
went through her. He could see the struggle she
was having. It was in the starkness of her gaze. He
could feel it in the death grip she had on him. "I
think maybe you should really, really kiss me."

"Yeah, I think so, too."

Sex, he reminded himself. That's what was going to happen here. They were going to have sex—

naked bodies, hot sheets, wet mouths—and just take the edge off what had become a very edgy night.

Gently tilting her head back, he grazed her cheek with his thumb, and closed the scant distance between them by thrusting his tongue into her mouth, slowly, deeply—and that's when he knew he was in so much fucking trouble.

He liked his sex hot and sweet, a little bit dirty when he could get it, and utterly shameless, just like those sorority girl sex games, and he didn't have a doubt in his mind that Honey could give him all those things, because she instantly melted against him in the way that got guys so hard, and one of her hands had tunneled up into his hair, pulling him down to her, like maybe he might get away if she didn't hold on to him, and her other hand was flat on the small of his back, holding him so close, pressing against him.

It was all that—the whole kiss, the moving of their mouths with each other, and with him not forgetting for a second that her shirt was completely unbuttoned and that her breasts were just a short slide of his hand away from where he was holding her at her waist.

It was all that, and more, and it wasn't even close to being enough.

He needed to be inside her.

Yeah. Kiss me, Smith, make me forget that woman is losing her mind out there.

She hadn't said "Fuck me, Smith, and make me forget everything." But that's what he was going to do.

Being careful with her butt, he lifted her up with his arm across the backs of her thighs, which made the front of her body absolutely plastered to the front of his—and that part didn't change, not for an instant. He heard one of her shoes drop onto the floor as he carried her across the room, still kissing her, then the other one. Just as well; she wasn't going to need her shoes, though sometimes that could be a nice little twist. She was still melted up against him when he took her down on the mattress with him on top.

And he just kept kissing her and kissing her, taking her mouth again and again, sliding his tongue over and around hers, sucking on her, and pushing aside her clothes, while she was doing the same thing to him, pushing his blue parrot shirt off his shoulders and dragging it down his arms before letting it fall to the bed.

His T-shirt went next with a quick grab and pull over his head, and then he had her halfway where he wanted her, with her bare breasts pressed against his chest.

Heavenly. She was so freaking soft, and so lush

and full. He bent his head down and took her breast in his mouth and sucked on her, and he felt her twist against him, her whole body rising toward his mouth, wanting more, trying to get even closer, both her hands tunneling through his hair.

He helped her along, reaching down and unbuttoning the cargo pants she was wearing and sliding his hand inside. The pants were big on her, giving him plenty of room to find his way, and when he did, she let out a soft sound of pleasure that got an instant reaction out of him. He rubbed his erection against her, then again, and the more he played with her, and the wetter she got, the harder he got.

When he felt her hands at his belt, he helped her there, too, rising off of her enough for the two of them to get his pants open and down off his hips. He brought one of his feet up so he could unlace his boot. He could make love with his pants on. He'd done it a few times, quickies here and there, but he wanted to get deep into Honey, the deeper the better.

With his boot gone and his pants off one leg, he was calling it good. It didn't take much to have her out of the other pair of cargoes, and at that point, to his credit, he did notice that he wasn't feeling very goddamn philosophical.

Not one bit.

No way.

Hot was about all he felt, hot and hard.

He rubbed his cock against her, teasing them both, fitting himself to her, and when she opened her legs a little wider, he took it as an open invitation to thrust.

God, she was silky and wet, and so help him God, when he pushed even deeper up inside her, she contracted around him. *Oh, yeah. Oh, geezus, yeah.*

He wrapped one hand around her thigh, pulling her closer, thrusting again and again, and a bolt of heat went straight down the middle of him. God, she felt so damn good, and her skin was soft, and she smelled so good.

Cupping her face with his other palm, he kissed her cheek, licked her lips, ran his tongue up the side of her neck. Her mouth came down open on his shoulder, her teeth grazing him, her hips moving against him with every stroke of his body, and man, he could have done it all night long like that, with Honey moving against him, and her body all soft and warm, endless moment after endless moment.

But then she whispered in his ear, and he felt the heat pushing him on harder. Reaching down between their bodies, he found the soft center of her arousal and teased her, gently stroking her, and the longer he did it, the sweeter it all got, achingly sweet.

Do me, Smith, she'd whispered. *Take me with you. Take me away.*

So far away, so deep inside her, deep inside himself. When she came, he was kissing her, his tongue in her mouth, tasting her, feeling her body contract around him. He thrust once more, harder, deeper, burying himself inside her, and he held himself there, his whole body shaking with the force of his release.

"WELL, THAT TOOK about five minutes to go straight to hell," Hawkins said over his radio.

Not about five, exactly five.

"Fuck," Dylan said, then thought it, just for the hell of it.

So much for all his well-laid plans for the night, all his running around like a goddamn chicken trying to keep all the other chickens out of trouble. Loretta had been right. SDF on the streets meant blood on the streets. *Shit.*

"Now, in our own defense," Hawkins continued, "let it be noted for the official record that we have the whole 'emergent threat' thing covered. Royce's guy drew first."

"And Red Dog aerated him."

"You know, Dylan, they're both damn good. Travis got a three-inch group and she got a clean heart shot on that boy, at night, in the rain, with only ambient light, using a pistol at forty meters."

"Where is she now?"

"Ahead of me, boss. She and Travis took cover in Sand Creek. Royce's other three guys followed them in. I'm three blocks behind them at the garage with the dead guy, and when I left Geiss Fastener, Zane Lowe and Royce were still in the Expedition, waiting things out. Waiting for somebody to bring them Red Dog, dead or alive, I'd bet."

"Hold on, I've got Grant on the line," Dylan said, catching Skeeter's signal. He picked up the phone. "Hart."

"I've got good news and bad news," Grant said.

"Give me the bad news."

"She not only visited Royce's place in San Luis, she tagged his walls with *Red Dog three-oh-three*."

Dylan refrained from a sigh, but sometimes, just sometimes, he felt like he was in charge of a bunch of juvenile delinquents. That's the way Steele Street had started, him and a crew of teenaged boys with nothing but time on their hands and getting into trouble on their minds—and sometimes it didn't seem like things had changed much.

"Obviously, it took him all of about two seconds to decode that one," Grant finished.

"And Rydell?"

"In the middle of a riot. San Luis is burning tires in her streets tonight. I checked with State, and there's a rebel group up in the mountains trying to stir things up again on the coast, oust the new *presidente*, the sort of thing El Salvador had hoped it had outgrown. State's not putting any odds on this rebel group. It's made up mostly of the farmers displaced by the new coffee consortium put together by the government, a few actual military types, with the whole thing backed by an overly politicized faction of the Catholic church."

"Is Rydell going to be able to get out of there in the morning?"

C. Smith Rydell was scheduled to be at Steele Street tomorrow night for a debriefing of the Panama mission.

"If he has to swim, he's out of there, according to him."

"Then I'll expect him." One thing Rydell could do was swim, with a wounded and bleeding partner under one arm, up a flooded river, with piranhas on their asses the whole way, according to Kid Chaos, a guy not given to exaggeration of any kind. Kid was a sniper. "Accuracy" was his mantra, and he meant one hundred percent. He worked with the facts. "What's the good news?"

"I've got your finding. State is taking a step away from Royce. The DEA has decided they'll be better off without him, and the CIA is just plain tired of him being an embarrassment to their fine organization. If you don't take him out, they will."

"So now we're doing the CIA's dirty work for them?" *Jesus.* What next? Dylan wondered. There was no such thing as a clean deal in this line of work, but sometimes, it got a little messy even for him.

"Take him out, Dylan," Grant said, his voice growing sober. It was an order, not a request. "He should have been ours two years ago."

Yes, he sure as hell should have been.

"Yes, sir." Tony Royce wouldn't be leaving Denver alive.

CHAPTER

26

WHAT DO YOU MEAN Johnson is dead?" Royce said from inside the big-ass SUV he'd rented at the airport, yelling into his phone. "You've only been gone for a goddamn half hour."

"He's dead, sir. He's got four holes in him, one through the heart," his man, Orlin, said.

Fuck. He should have brought more men. He would have thought that five of the meanest son of a bitches in the world would be enough to take out one slightly deranged, five-foot, five-inch woman.

"And where the hell is his body?" Royce hadn't planned on dragging any dead bodies home, for Chrissakes.

"Close to her apartment at the garage."

"Strip him of any identification, and I mean any

goddamn piece of whatnot the asshole has on him. Let the Denver cops figure out who he is." Goddamn Johnson, getting his ass waxed in under an hour. Maybe Royce needed to reevaluate his recruiting procedures.

When he didn't get an immediate answer from Orlin, he felt another shitty piece of news heading his way.

"What?" he demanded. He didn't like to be kept in suspense.

"They got to the body first," Orlin said.

"Who?"

"SDF."

"How?" he snapped. "If you were with fucking Johnson, and he was shooting at her, what the fuck did she do? Walk into your line of fire to get at him?"

Her medical report said she was tough, physically enhanced, but she wasn't bulletproof. She wasn't freaking Superman.

But somebody was.

Shit.

"We were flanked. Somebody was shooting at us from behind."

And Orlin had the balls to admit it, or the stupidity. Royce wasn't sure which, but something had suddenly become crystal fucking clear.

"You better keep your head about you, Orlin, or

you won't make it, either. Christian Hawkins is on your ass. Now get out there, and get me that girl."

Goddammit. Royce shut his phone, then pulled his Springfield out of his shoulder holster and checked the load. *Goddammit.*

Skeeter Bang was a dangerous bitch. *Geezus.* She'd taken his fucking eyeball right out of his head.

Her boy toy, Dylan Hart, had been a razor-sharp thorn in Royce's side for more years than he cared to remember. Royce had done his damnedest to kill the guy two or three times and hadn't been able to pull it off.

Creed Rivera and Kid Chaos Chronopolous were relentless, especially on the hunt, two sides of the same ruthlessly dangerous coin—hot and cold, wild and controlled.

And Christian Hawkins was Superman, the one SDF operator Royce avoided like the plague. He'd always stayed away from Hawkins's missions, even when he'd been with the CIA. The guy wasn't more brutal than the other operators. He wasn't tougher, or meaner, or more dangerous with a gun—it seemed Red Dog was garnering that designation.

But Christian Hawkins was something— something Royce hadn't quite been able to put his finger on, and that bugged the fuck out of him. It unnerved him in a way he resented, but hadn't been able to change, not in all the years he'd been tracking Special Defense Force.

So he stayed away from the guy.

And the last goddamn thing he wanted to know was that Superman was out there in the dark, somewhere close, patrolling the streets and backing up Gillian Pentycote.

He looked to Zane, sitting behind the wheel of the Expedition, on the radio with one of their guys.

"You're sharp tonight, right? Ready for anything?"

Zane looked over at him and nodded. "Yes, sir," he said.

He better be.

"Good," Royce said. "You just stay sharp."

Zane nodded again.

Good, Royce thought. *Good*. But somehow it didn't make him feel any goddamn better.

TRAVIS had one goal, to stay behind Gillian and still keep up with her. *Geezus*, she was running like a freaking gazelle. They both knew Sand Creek like the backs of their hands, and he'd given her an unmistakable signal to get her ass down into the creek bed.

With the first shot, Royce's men had made

themselves fair targets. Nobody was going to get fried for killing any of the Damn Dirty Dozen, but the vacant lots stretching between the garage and the dry creek didn't offer much cover. There were still at least three guys in the streets behind them, and that was if Zane Lowe had stayed with Royce at Geiss Fastener.

Hawkins hadn't vouched for Zane's whereabouts. Superman was on the other side of the garage, in the alley trying to lock onto the positions of Royce's men. They'd deployed from the Expedition, not traveling as a pack, and the only one Hawkins had pinpointed was the one he'd followed, the one Travis and Gillian had killed.

Geezus, what a beautiful shot she'd made. And she'd gotten it off before he'd hardly let go of her.

Nobody was that fast.

Nobody.

And the way she was running. *Fuck*. Something was wrong, and it scared the hell out of him.

Her body was such a mystery, sleek and lean, and unpredictable. Tonight, when she'd come, she'd gotten so hot. He'd loved it, but in the back of his mind, he'd known it wasn't right, wasn't good, not for her temperature to rise that much, that quickly.

She dove for a hole in the fence, and he was right behind her, sliding under the chain link and dropping down the bank into the section of the creek they called the Junkyard. Dumpsters, abandoned cars, a couple of freight containers, there was even a junked walk-in cooler. It was all great cover from freaking paintballs, but Royce's men had pulled subguns and pistols out of the back of the Expedition.

Those assholes, to come gunning for his girlfriend.

He'd said "Yes, sir," to Dylan, and he'd meant it. He'd understood from the beginning what it took to be a member of SDF, and he knew what it took to live with himself, and he knew enough to take himself off the team, if he ever doubted on what side of those lines he stood.

It had happened once before, an SDF operator taking himself off the team. Zachary Prade, one of the original chop-shop boys, had done it, walked away and dropped off the edge of the earth. No one had ever said why, but Travis didn't think it had been because of a woman, and certainly not a woman like Red Dog—because there had never been another woman like Red Dog.

She was headed toward the Fort, two freight containers that had been piled on top of each other, with an observation post they'd rigged on top of the mound of metal. They had time to scramble up the containers before any of Royce's men could have had a chance to get behind them. At the top, they took cover behind a slab of steel plate Johnny Ramos had welded together. The plate had a hole cut out of the middle of it. Travis slid into place behind it and caught his breath.

Gillian wasn't even breathing hard.

Rain was running down everything, pooling on top of the container.

She pulled her Contender out of its holster inside her vest, then quickly made a roll of material out of her Nomex hood and her fast-rope gloves and laid the roll on the "sill" of the steel plate. Resting the Contender with its .223 barrel on top of the material, she took up her firing position.

They both knew the distance from the Fort to everything they could see. It had all been measured with a laser range finder many times. With the .223, there wasn't much out there that she could see that she couldn't "reach out and touch" real up close and personal with her pistol.

Still, he was surprised at the speed with which she acquired a new target and took a shot. The boattail bullets flew at well over Mach 2 and produced a loud sonic *crack* along the entire trajectory that, close up, was almost loud enough to drown out the muzzle blast.

It rung his chimes.

"Tell Gillian thank you," Hawkins said in his ear a couple of seconds later.

Hell.

"Who'd she get?"

"Whoever was on my ass," Hawkins said. "I'll go take a look."

"Matchsticks," Dylan had called these guys, and Travis was beginning to understand exactly what he'd meant.

He wasn't inclined to tell her to shoot less, and yet the night had barely begun and she'd already killed two men, and he wasn't sure how she'd even found that last damn target—not as quickly as she had.

He pulled a pair of compact binoculars out of his vest and scanned the streets and buildings on either side of the SDF garage.

"Where are you?" he asked Hawkins, keying his mic.

"On the south side of Thompson's Body Shop. You've still got at least two guys out here, some-where."

"The south side?" He knew the body shop, and if Superman was on the south side of it, he was headed away from the fight.

"We've been given a green light on Royce," Superman said. "From Grant himself. I'm doubling back to Geiss Fastener, before Gillian spooks him into next week."

Travis understood. Heavy losses so quickly at the beginning of the fight might make the man decide to cut and run, and Royce was the real prize here tonight, not his goons. He needed to be neutralized, permanently. Royce had tracked Gillian right to her home base in Commerce City. She wouldn't be safe anywhere from here on out. Travis did not want him to get away, not when he was within range and General Grant had sanctioned his termination.

He lifted his face away from the binoculars and glanced at Gillian. She wanted the hit. She'd made this all happen here tonight, and she would want to be the one to take out Royce.

They could run the creek bed and come out within a block of the Geiss parking lot. If Royce's other two guys wanted to try to follow them through the Junkyard, it was going to be the last bad decision they made.

"We'll follow Sand Creek," he said to Hawkins, checking the neighborhood through his binoculars again. "We'll come up on Enright Street, and head straight south to Geiss and meet you there."

"I'm on Burgess," Hawkins said. "And I'll let you know if that changes. You'll see my Sheila on Enright."

At Steele Street, a "Sheila" was any of the highly maintained but completely nondescript cars they used when a low profile was important.

Skeeter had given him Adeline, who was anything but nondescript, but Travis knew she'd done it for a reason, and as long as Travis got Addy home in one piece, there wouldn't be a problem. Quinn would never begrudge the death of a car to save a teammate—but Quinn did love his cars.

"Roger," he said to Hawkins, keying his mic. Then he looked at Gillian. She didn't know Royce was in the neighborhood. She didn't know Hawkins had been on his tail since he'd landed in Denver—and part of Travis wanted to keep it that way.

But that option really wasn't available. They were in this fight together, whether he liked it or not. There was no way to leave her behind, no safe way.

Looking at her, he was still so angry he could hardly see straight—but that was all going to have to wait. They had one job right now, a job made up of two very specific tasks: Kill the bad guys, and survive.

H E HAD A TATTOO.

It was the last thing Honey would have expected, that C. Smith Rydell would have a tattoo, especially a cosmic tattoo, but there it was, a fiery, blazing sunburst on his left shoulder. He was asleep on his stomach, which was giving her the absolute best view she'd ever had of a naked man.

Most men were not built like C. Smith, not even close. Even the guys she knew who worked out were a bit lacking. Their muscles were as big, which meant they were very big, but the guys she knew could not be classified as rugged, except possibly her oldest brother, who managed to get out in the world and take it on a bit.

Rydell took it on a lot. The truth was in every

line of his body, in the truly impressive curve of his biceps, in the beard-stubbled angle of his jaw, in the hard, muscular length of his legs. He was beautiful, possibly the most beautiful man she'd ever seen, and she'd actually dated a Calvin Klein underwear model once.

The tattoo fit him. God knew, she felt like she'd been dipped in fiery, blazing sunlight—and that was just the sex. The way he'd held her afterward had been a whole other level of comfort and warmth, and definitely of cosmic proportions. It all made her wonder if she should have tried a one-night stand earlier in life. He was her first, and for sheer, mind-blowing, orgasmic power, he'd gone straight to the top of her very short list of lovers.

She was going to be thinking about him in the years to come, she could guarantee it, and maybe he would think about her. She finished signing her copy of *The Sorority Girl's Guide to Self-Help Sex*: To C. Smith Rydell, with love and fondest memories. Honoria York-Lytton.

Possibly the "fondest memories" part was a little overdone, but she didn't want him to think she hadn't enjoyed their time together—enjoyed it the way she enjoyed breathing and dark-chocolate-dipped cherries.

She brought her fingers to her temple, closed her eyes, and took a breath. One-night stand. God, what a shame. She would love to make love with him again, oh, maybe a few hundred times.

She took another breath and shook the feeling off. Being sad for something that never should have been and had the cosmic probability of a gnat's chances in hell of ever happening again was ridiculous. She knew what people thought when they first met her, that she was cute, and possibly, probably vacuous, that the York-Lytton money negated any necessity of her ever using her brain. She knew what she looked like, especially in her girly-girl couture. She spent a helluva lot of money to look the way she did. For her to leave the house without at least five hundred dollars' worth of whatever hanging off of her had never happened, ever, and a thousand or more was more usual. She was expensive, high-maintenance, and worth every penny. She didn't doubt it for a second.

And she'd just made love—had sex, she corrected herself—with a guy whose most expensive accessory was his gun.

The gun he'd left on the nightstand.

Oh.

She was headed out the door into the scary night, and lo and behold, there was a gun.

He had bullets. Tons of them.

Of course, it was wrong to steal his gun, but

faced with necessity, she could be very practical—criminally practical.

She fished a bundle of fifties out of her tote and peeled off a thousand dollars' worth. She owed him five for the bodyguarding, the best five hundred dollars she'd ever spent. He was very good at it. The clothes she was taking couldn't possibly have cost a hundred dollars, but she was paying him a hundred for them anyway.

And now she was stealing his gun. He'd probably paid quite a bit for it, but she didn't have a clue how much. She'd leave him the four hundred and either send the gun back to him or send him more money when she found out how much a weapon like his cost.

So maybe she should go through his wallet, so she'd know how to contact him.

Sure she should, she thought, looking over at him.

It was all so obvious now, she wondered that she hadn't thought of it right off the bat. If nothing else, she'd like a confirmation on his name. "Smith" just didn't set right. Who named their child Smith? And what did that C stand for?

He let out a soft snore, but without moving another muscle on his entire body, so she wasn't too worried. The man was practically out cold. Sex had that effect on men sometimes. A lot of the time.

Without an ounce of guilt, she searched his pants until she felt his wallet, but when she stuck her hand in his pocket, the wallet wasn't there. It seemed to be in another pocket altogether. So she felt around some more, until she figured out that there was a secret pocket inside his pocket, and there was a secret zipper under a secret flap.

Who was this guy? she wondered—but not for long.

Once she pulled his wallet out and opened it up, she knew he hadn't lied to her about his name, unless he was traveling under a very well put-together false identity. Every piece of identification he had, and he had a bunch, said he was C. Smith Rydell, including his Colorado driver's license.

She liked Colorado, especially Aspen and Vail, which were the only two places she'd ever been in Colorado, the only two places anybody she knew had ever been. He was from Denver, which she was sure was very nice, and his address was 738 Steele Street, which she memorized in a heartbeat.

That was really all she needed.

But she'd just had the most amazing sex of her life with this guy, and she was never going to see him after she left the Hotel Palacio, so she just went ahead and pried—big-time.

He snored again, and she looked over at him. God, he'd felt so good inside her. She hadn't known a man could feel that good. Maybe it was the way he'd been kissing her at the same time, or the way he'd been holding her, or the way he'd smelled, or the way he'd tasted. It had all been so good.

Or maybe it was just the heat, and the night, and the danger making him so fascinating.

She let out a sigh and went back to going through his wallet, flipping through one piece of paper at a time. He had some interesting stuff. Money, of course, U.S. dollars and Salvadoran *colones*. He also had a VIP pass to the Hotel Panama, a guest receipt to the Palacio, and a TACA boarding pass from Panama City to Ilopongo, the airport in San Salvador.

So the whole Panama thing hadn't been a lie, either.

He had a couple of other official-looking IDs, one from something called IRIS, the Institute for Regional and International Studies, with his photo on it, designating him as a Public Safety Instructor for Central America, and requesting that all local authorities honor his permission to carry a concealed firearm for his personal defense.

With all the traveling she did, she needed one of those, to keep from ever having to buy a gun from some guy off the street named Hector ever again. She really did have a lot of friends at the State

Department. Maybe one of them could get her an IRIS. ID.

Another minute of searching revealed a U.S. State Department Visitor's Pass, but no employment ID, which didn't surprise her. He'd changed his story to the Department of Defense, but there wasn't anything in his wallet so far that identified him as working for the DOD either, and there was no military ID. He did have two business cards, both for women, one at the embassy in Guatemala City, the other at the Sheraton in San Salvador, which she really had no business even thinking about, let alone wondering about, like wondering if they knew how good he was in bed, too.

Don't, she told herself. Just don't. He was a one-night stand, whose wallet she was going through like he was an unfaithful husband.

She ought to be ashamed, and as soon as she saw Julia and knew her baby sister was as safe as she was likely to be, considering the company she kept, and the convictions she had, and as soon as Honey got home, and everything was back to normal, she'd be as ashamed as necessary.

Until then, she was looking, and what she found next was possibly the most interesting thing he had, a hand-sketched map showing the location of an airstrip outside San Luis. Yessirree, everybody needed one of those, right along with permission to carry a weapon in a foreign country.

My, oh my, Mr. Rydell truly was mysterious, which just made him all that much more fascinating. But she had a name and an address, and that was all she needed. It was time for her to leave, past time.

Tucking his wallet back into his secret pocket, she allowed her gaze to go over him one more time. She wished she could kiss him good-bye, but that was out of the question. She needed to sneak off, and kissing was not sneaking.

Two miles, that's all she had to do: get two miles through a riot-torn city from the Hotel Palacio to the sacristy at St. Mary's.

Scooting off the bed, she grabbed her tote and, as quietly as possible, made her way to the door. The locks slid smoothly out of place, and wearing baggy boy clothes and white platform heels, she slipped out onto the veranda and into the night.

CHAPTER

28

"WHO'S ON the radio?" Gillian asked, reloading her Contender out of her cartridge cuff.

The rain was increasing in strength, turning colder, and there'd been some lightning off to the east.

She knew Royce's men, knew them all by heart, their faces, their crimes, the way each of them worked. She knew their vices, and knew none of them had any virtues, and she'd just killed two of them—Johnson and Graham.

The world was suddenly a better place.

"Superman," Travis said.

"Good."

He was still angry. She could feel it pulsing off of him, but they had a job to do, and everything else was put aside until it was done. That was professional, and they'd always made a good team professionally.

A better team personally, she'd always thought, and maybe she'd ruined that forever. All these years, all the crap they'd been through, and she really hadn't known he could be pushed to fury, not Angel.

She'd been wrong, and the fact brought her up short, made her think.

"Why are we meeting him at Geiss?" The fastener company had been out of business for years, but something was obviously going on over there.

"Royce is there, in a black Expedition, waiting for his guys to bring you in. Zane Lowe is with him."

For a second, she didn't hear anything beyond Royce.

He was here.

In Commerce City, within reach.

Everything in her stopped for an instant, then started up faster. The monster was here.

Here.

A sick, winding rope of fear twisted in her gut, and her skin suddenly felt cold.

Here.

"You don't have to go," Angel said.

Yes, she did.

There was no other way.

But a tremor had just slid up her arm, and her breath was becoming a little short.

"Gillian?"

"I'm fine. Really." She closed the action on the Contender and slid it back in its holster.

"We've got to move. We can't stay here."

She didn't want to stay at the Fort. She wanted to run in the opposite direction of Geiss, but there was no hope for her that way.

A short burst of subgun fire had them both dropping even closer to the freight container, keeping their heads down. The rounds hit a Dumpster a good twenty yards to the north of them, the ping of the bullets telling them both that Royce's men were firing blind.

"We can wait and take them," she said.

He shook his head. "Royce is going to know he's losing men. We either go get him now, or we risk the chance of him running."

"So how many of his guys are out there?"

"We're down to two here, and Lowe and Royce at Geiss."

"And we've got Hawkins with us. Anybody else?"

"Skeeter and Dylan are at Steele Street."

And it was time for them to go, past time.

"Enright?" she said, and he nodded.

"We'll take it east out of the creek bed and come in right on top of them. Hawkins is coming up Burgess Street."

It was a clean plan, a good plan. Angel would be with her, and Hawkins would be on her right when they hit Enright Street.

The rattling of a chain-link fence up ahead of them became the signal to go. Keeping low and in line with the steel shield, Angel moved to the back of the freight container and dropped to the ground.

She was right behind him, and together they took off up the creek bed, weaving a well-known path through a landscape of abandoned cars and containers. Thirty more yards to the south, the junk and cars created a funnel, a three-yard-wide opening along the front of a Dumpster shoved up against a pile of junk, tires, and old washing machines too dense to get through.

Angel signaled her, and she took up a guard position next to the Dumpster as he quickly rigged a trip-line with a length of parachute cord.

There was a lot of trash, spills, broken glass, and just plain bad stuff in the creek bed, and landing in it face first was guaranteed to be either toxic or bloody.

He tied off the cord, the whole process taking mere seconds, and they took off again at a run.

———

"GRAHAM?"

"Yes, sir."

Royce didn't want to hear it.

"You guys are smarter than that. You're better than that." That's why he paid them what the hell he paid them. They were not supposed to drop like flies.

He had a pretty good record against SDF. Informing the National Revolutionary Forces, a narco-guerilla group in Colombia, about the CIA's impending actions against them and the incursion of a pair of Special Defense Force operators into their territory had gotten J. T. Chronopolous massacred and netted Royce a guaranteed foothold in their cartel-connected cocaine pipeline, a purely business transaction that had been the basis for his independent launch into the worldwide drug trade.

The kidnapping and subsequent torture of Dylan Hart on the island of Sumba in Indonesia by Royce's former heroin trade associate, Hamzah Negara, had been one of the highlights of his career.

Watching Dr. Souk terrify and torture Gillian Pentycote had paled in comparison to the show Hart had put on. The man had suffered, and Royce had relished every moment, every spastic twist of his body, every strangled scream.

But tonight was Pentycote's night, the bitch, and she was killing his men like they were Cub Scouts.

And Superman was out there, somewhere.

"Have you seen Hawkins?"

"No, sir."

"And who is this other guy Peters told me is with her?"

"We think it's Travis James."

"The asshole who waxed that pair of Colombians on the coast last year?" It hadn't been a hit. It had been a deal that had gone bad, where the suppliers involved had screwed up, then tried to salvage an unsalvageable mess by going after the SDF guys who had fucked them over in the first place. It was the last hunting trip either of them had ever taken.

"Yes, sir."

Royce knew things. He was connected. His twenty-five years with the CIA had given him a network of informants, government officials, criminal bosses, warlords, drug lords, and English lords who sent information his way from every corner of the earth.

Royce knew things, but he did not know how these goddamn SDF women kept kicking his ass.

He lifted his hand to his face and felt the scar that ran from his forehead down to his jaw. His eye hurt, the one that wasn't even fucking there.

Sometimes he thought about retirement. Not the kind the Feds would like to give him, but a real retirement, with a beach and a boat. San Luis was the beginning of that dream. A villa to make other men pant with envy, a quiet town, tropical weather. Maybe he'd grow coffee beans. The Salvadoran government had just made coffee growing a profitable business venture, if a man's business was big enough.

Royce's business was very big.

And he was going to give Orlin and crew about another half an hour to tie this thing up, and then he was leaving. He was not hanging around a potential disaster just to see how it turned out, or on the off chance that his men might accidentally pull out a victory.

One more dead guy, and Royce was leaving.

GILLIAN'S blood was running hot and fast, pumping through her veins. She could feel it. The night was getting clearer to her, even through the rain, brighter, starker, turning black and white at the edges if she moved her head too quickly.

It was all new, unprecedented, unlike any of the

other symptoms she'd suffered through over the years. Most intriguing of all was that it wasn't disturbing. She felt stronger, faster, even though she could tell Angel was slowly outdistancing her.

Royce, the monster, was up ahead, lying in wait, and she knew exactly what he wanted: more of what he'd already gotten out of her—terror and pain.

She was going to give him both.

So she ran with the Angel toward doom.

The night slid by her on either side, the blacks and whites streaking into gray. It didn't matter.

There were men coming up behind her. She could hear them now, when she hadn't been able to hear them before. The clatter of their feet through piles of trash, the laboring of their breath through the pace Angel was setting. They wanted her the same way she wanted Royce.

She wiped at the rain on her face and kept running.

When they reached the low bank at Enright Street, the two of them scrambled up onto the ditch road. It was a dangerous crossing, where they would be exposed for precious seconds until they reached the darkness and cover of the buildings on the other side.

The men were very close now. She could almost smell them.

Angel dropped to one knee at the edge of a junked car and fired off a short burst.

A man cried out, but Gillian just kept running. Once on the other side of the road, she dropped to her knee and provided cover for Angel. They were a team.

When he caught up to her, she rose to her feet again, and in the split second between when she stood up and turned to run, something slammed into her. She stumbled, but then righted herself and kept going.

At the corner of the street, she glanced up and read the words "Enright Street." They were on track. All she had to do was run.

CHAPTER

29

─◇─

"THIS IS A DONE DEAL, Dylan," Hawkins said, his voice no more than a whisper into his mic.

"Where are Travis and Gillian?"

"Don't know, boss. I heard gunfire one minute ago, and Travis confirmed another of Royce's guys hit. He thought it was a good hit and the guy was dead. A few seconds later, there were more shots fired, but I didn't hear from him on those. I should have a visual on them real quick. He didn't answer my last signal."

"Do you have Royce and Lowe in sight?"

"Affirmative. Both targets are inside the SUV."

"Then do the CIA a favor."

Hawkins wiped the rain from his face and moved across the alley to improve his firing position. He'd always wanted this moment to be a little more personal, but he wasn't going to complain. Royce was his.

Tucking himself up against a brick wall, he raised his HK UMP45, automatically adjusting his point of aim to take the car windows into account. He was going to take Lowe out first, because he was the driver, then Royce's choices would be narrowed down a bit. He could sit in his seat and take what happened next, or he could bail.

Either option worked for Hawkins.

His first burst went as planned—almost. Without being able to see inside the darkened windows through the rain, even though he'd prayed for a direct hit on the bastard, he didn't get it. The windshield shattered, and the car lurched forward.

Hawkins rose to his feet, still shooting, but didn't leave the cover of the building. Without the windshield his chances of hitting Lowe had improved, or they would have if Royce's lieutenant hadn't floored the Expedition.

He immediately adjusted his aim to the tires, and took two of them out in seconds. Then he shot the rest of the windows.

He could hear Travis on his headset again, trying to confirm his position so he could add more firepower to the situation as soon as they got within sight of the parking lot.

Enright Street was to Hawkins's left, and he moved in that direction, still firing on the Expedition. There was still one other of Royce's men out in the night, and Superman didn't forget it for a second.

The car was not only still moving, it was picking up speed, and headed down Enright. Goddamn Lowe was proving hard to kill, and if Hawkins didn't get the job done pretty damn quick, he was going to find himself out of this fight. He really needed to hit something significant in the next couple of seconds.

He must have, from the rear, no less, because the SUV made a sudden right turn and plowed into a truck parked on Enright.

"Coming down Enright," he said into his mic. "Hugging the walls on the south side. The SUV is crashed on the north side, the passenger door opening."

He gave it a burst, and then a barrage of gunfire came pouring out of the SUV. Hawkins slid back behind a wall. As soon as the firing was over, he took a quick peek, and realized things were going to get a lot more personal than he'd thought.

"Lowe heading in your direction. Do you copy?"

"Affirmative."

And Royce was his. The bastard had just

disappeared up the alley between Geiss Fastener and a boarded-up hardware store.

"Where's the last guy who followed you into Sand Creek?" It would be a good thing to know.

"DEAD." Travis said the word into his headset, and Gillian knew he was talking about the man she'd just killed. It had been one shot, center chest, at fifty meters with her TC.

They ducked into the nearest alley, and that's when she realized she'd been hurt. Her left shoulder was almost numb, and yet it ached.

She looked at it and saw blood staining her assault vest.

"What happened?" Travis asked when they stopped. He looked both ways, up and down the alley, and so did she. There was nothing at either end.

"I got hit," she said, leaning against the wall. Her stomach was churning, and sweat was pouring down her face, mixing with the rain. She wasn't feeling strong now.

"When?" They both knew the guy she'd just killed hadn't gotten a shot off.

"At the ditch road, when we crossed." When she'd felt something slam into her.

He swore under his breath.

"Stay put here," he said, slinging the shotgun off from over his head and handing it to her along with a handful of shells. "You've got plenty of ammo, right?"

"A lot," she confirmed, and wondered what in the hell was happening to her. She was really cold on the outside, and really hot on the inside, and it was making her feel sick.

But then she thought maybe she didn't want to know what was happening. Or maybe she did know, and this was it, and Angel was going to lose her while he was still so angry with her.

"I didn't do it to hurt you," she said. "None of it."

His gaze met hers, but it was hard to read, and that hurt as much as anything.

"I know," he said, but it didn't sound like it made any difference. "Look, Lowe and Royce are still out there, to the west of this position, and Lowe is headed this way. I'm going to cut him off."

"Was that the crash we heard?"

"Yeah, the SUV. That's why the two of them are on foot."

"Be careful."

"Stay put."

He moved back down to the end of the alley, and slipped back out onto the street.

God. She leaned her head against the brick wall at her back. The whole world was going black and white on her, and with every passing second, her left arm felt more and more useless, but maybe, if she got to the end of the alley, she could still provide him with some cover.

That was her plan.

But she'd no sooner pushed off the wall and taken a couple of halting steps than she was grabbed from behind by someone huge.

"You stupid bitch," a man's voice said, his arms tightening around her like a giant vise.

Geezus! Where in the holy hell had he come from?

She struggled, but the guy was a behemoth, lifting her off her feet like she was nothing, and that fact alone told her who had her in his grip: Zane Lowe, Royce's beast. He'd outflanked them, and it felt like he was planning on squeezing her to death. She could hardly breathe, and her left arm felt leaden. *Geezus.* He was like a freaking boa constrictor.

She wasn't used to feeling helpless, not anymore, not now, and it started a curl of panic inside her. She wasn't Gillian Pentycote. She was Red Dog, but it didn't matter, because the harder she struggled and the more she tried to fight, the tighter he held her. *Fuck.* She was seeing stars.

And then she was seeing Travis, and she no sooner saw him than she saw him draw his Glock and start down the alley, pistol raised. The whole action, from his first step until Zane Lowe dropped like a stone with her still in his arms, took less than a second.

Head shot. Clean. Fast. Deadly accurate.

It had to be, and if she'd had an ounce of strength left in her, she would have turned to look, but the night was closing in.

God. She dragged a breath into her lungs—and it hurt, just like everything else.

She'd failed.

Pushing herself off the dead mountain of a sonuvabitch, she rolled onto the ground. If she could just get to her feet, she thought, then she could breathe, she could steady herself.

But no matter what she did, she knew she wouldn't be killing the monster tonight. She was coming to an end, and he'd eluded her, like he always did in her mind, slipped behind one of those walls that she could never get around. Those walls hid his lair, and it was inside her, the place where he lurked and schemed and sent out his screams of pain.

God. She let out a gasp and rolled her shoulder into the wall.

If she could just get to her feet.

Pressing herself against the brick, she dug the

fingers of her other hand into the mortar and dragged one of her feet beneath her.

Inside her. Oh, God.

She slid her fingers up into the next line of mortar and pulled, using her leg to lift herself. With each inch she gained, she pressed herself harder into the wall, using it, and she gasped with the pain building up inside her.

"Shhh, baby. Shhh. I'm here." A pair of arms came around her, strong but gentle, helping her, sliding behind her back and under her legs, lifting her off her feet, away from the wall, and holding her close.

"Travis, I—" She wanted to hold on, to hold on to him, to hold on to herself, but she couldn't.

She was sliding inside, slipping away. She started to tremble—tremble and shake, right down to her veins, right down to her pulse, and her heart, and her bones.

"I've got you," he said, tightening his hold on her, his long strides taking her out of the alley and into the openness of the street.

"N-not this time, Angel." She was on her own, heading straight to hell. She could see it out there on the horizon, in stark black and white, waiting for her, beckoning, and Royce was waiting for her there.

Oh, God.

"I-I can't . . . you can't, I—"

"Fuck *can't*, babe," he growled. "Maybe you are going to run out on me again and again, and maybe I *won't* be there every time—but *this* time, Red Dog, *this* time, I've got you."

Her body started to spasm, the pain twisting inside her.

"Skeeter," she heard him say. "Skeeter, get me a medevac. One patient, adult female, semi-concious. Single gunshot wound, upper left thorax. Code red."

CHAPTER

30

ORPHANS, MY ASS, Smith thought, looking through a window into the St. Mary's sacristy.

If her butt hadn't already been hurting, he'd paddle her until she couldn't sit for a week, and why that was his responsibility, he didn't have a clue.

Except they'd had sex, great sex, and somehow, sometimes, that made him feel like he had a freaking relationship with a woman. It shouldn't.

Especially when that woman was handing over a quarter of a million dollars to a guy dressed in jungle BDUs, which just begged the question of what in the hell she was up to in the middle of the night in San Luis. He didn't really care what she did with her money, but if that guy was what he looked like, and people usually were, throwing it away on a Third World rebellion that was only going to get people killed and probably not accomplish a whole helluva lot of anything else pissed him off.

To her credit, possibly, and he was being generous here, she wasn't the one actually giving the guerilla the money. Stack by stack, it was going around the table from Honey, to a young woman who could only be Sister Julia—the resemblance was startling—to a priest, probably the Father Bartolo she'd mentioned, who was making notations in a ledger book, to the guy in green camo.

Yeah, it was just a simple, covert operation with a lot of money changing hands, just a little under-the-table funding of a bunch of thugs who didn't have any other way of making a living except to foment rebellion. If it had just been Honey, Julia, the good father, and the guy in green camo, Smith might have walked away and gone back to the Palacio to wait out the rest of the lousy night, until he could get on a plane out of San Luis and out of El Salvador.

But there were two other guys in the room, and if Honey wasn't nervous, she should have been. One of those guys hadn't taken his eyes off her since Smith had been watching through the window, and the other goon had an M4 carbine cradled in his arms, his finger damn close to the trigger.

The whole setup sucked.

And she'd stolen his gun.

So he was standing in the dark outside a Catholic church full of rebels, with nothing but an ancient pistol loaded with a single cartridge to keep bad things from happening.

It wasn't much.

Inside the room, the conversation seemed to come to a stop. The guy with the M4 gestured toward Honey's tote bag, and she responded by holding it close to her body, which was a real bad sign, and probably not the wisest course of action.

If she'd talked this whole thing out with him, instead of lying about little orphans with broken arms, he would have told her to never take anything into one of these meetings that you weren't willing to give up or put on the table. Clutching goodies to your chest only made the bad guys want them all that much more—a point proven when M4 guy started around the table, heading for her.

He didn't get far. Both the nun and the priest rose to their feet in protest, gesturing, and the guy in green camo said something that stopped M4 guy in his tracks.

Smith didn't move, just watched.

With the money already on the table, even if the

guy grabbed her tote, Honey would only be out some fingernail polish and half a dozen melted candy bars. The problem would be if the guy with the M4 grabbed her, because then, standing around outside and watching was not going to be an option.

The door at the far end of the room opened, and Smith tightened his grip on the ancient pistol, bringing it to a low ready position. During his years with the DEA, he'd been in a few situations with piles of money on a table and a bunch of bad assholes standing around counting it. Some of those situations had not turned out well.

So he was ready for anything.

Ready for anything except the little old nun who came into the room carrying a pot of food.

Okay. He could do nuns and food. He lowered the pistol back to his side but stayed on alert.

When a priest came in with a steaming casserole dish, he relaxed another degree. By the third nun with food, he'd uncocked the pistol.

The situation inside the room was starting to look like a family gathering, and he liked it. He liked it a lot. Food was a good thing. So was smiling, and green camo guy was smiling. M4 guy still looked pissed, but he was eating, and eating was good. Most people did not start shooting things while they were eating, even guys with M4s. The guy who couldn't take his eyes off Honey was still staring at her, but he was eating, too, and he could look all he wanted.

He could not touch.

Touching was no good.

Smith didn't let anybody touch him, and he wasn't going to take it too kindly if the jerk touched Honey. It was really none of his business, except the guy had no business touching her.

Come to think of it, Smith probably hadn't had any business touching her himself. That was a quarter of a million dollars that had just changed hands, and she'd dragged it into the country like a handful of pocket change.

No, he was pretty sure he hadn't had any business touching her—and he'd done a whole lot more than that.

Given half a chance, he'd do it over again, all of it, but he really didn't see half a chance anywhere on the horizon, and he wasn't going to get maudlin about it.

He was going to think about it, though, probably quite a bit in the next few months, and he knew he was going to wish it had all taken a whole lot longer than it had, and that they'd had a chance to put their heads together and come up with a few shameless, sorority girl sex games to play.

That would have been fun.

Hell. He leaned against the wall and checked the room again. She and her sister were sitting close together, holding on to each other, with Honey's arm wrapped around the younger woman's waist while they ate, and smiled, and talked. Every now and then he saw Honey reach up to wipe a tear from her face, which made him damn glad all he had were a bunch of hard-ass brothers to put up with. A do-gooding saint for a sister sacrificing herself in a Third World country would have tried his patience to the breaking point.

Dessert was brought out next, and coffee, and the food was looking really damn good to him, especially the coffee.

When they brought the orphans in, though, that's what really tore it for him. One after another, the kids trooped in under the guidance of a nun who looked like keeping children in line was her calling, and one by one, they all went up and said something to Honey. Shy, cute, and scrubbed clean, watching them introduce themselves to her shot him right back into that Shirley Temple movie. As each one finished, they went straight to Julia, and he could tell by the expression on her face, and especially by the expressions on the children's faces, that she was telling them how well they'd done, and how proud she was of them, and he knew for a fact that every little girl in the room wanted to grow up to be a nun, and every little boy was in love with her—especially the one with his arm in a cast.

No shit, even that had been true.

Hell, by the time the last child had trooped back out, he was half in love with Sister Julia himself. She was Honey's sister, no doubt, with a sweetly delicate pixie face and green eyes—and when the light caught her just so, she looked radiant, like maybe she really was a saint, which he figured pretty much finished up the night for him.

Honey was fine, and he was done. Nothing in that room was going to hurt anybody tonight. A quarter of a million dollars could do a lot of good, or a lot of harm, and it wasn't always easy to see which way it was going to go with money and good intentions—but none of that was going to happen tonight.

Turning his back on the church, he started walking. At the street, he looked both ways, not for traffic—there was none—but for whatever was left of the riots. There wasn't much, a burning pile of trash at one end, and a few stragglers at the other. Whatever the whole goddamn night had been about, he'd catch it on CNN.

Shameless sorority girl sex games—*geezus*. He grinned and crossed the street.

CHAPTER

31

HAWKINS LIKED to hunt—men. Other than that, he pretty much kept to a life of fine art appreciation and serious, hands-on fathering. He had two kids already on board and another in the hamper, and life was sweet.

And he still liked hunting men, especially men who were returning the favor.

Royce was a wily old fox, with "old" being the most pertinent adjective in the current situation. Still, the ex-CIA agent was armed and dangerous, and Hawkins wasn't taking any chances on missing any birthdays, ever, so he was running the old guy into the ground.

Royce could have stopped and taken another stand, but they both knew how that was going to turn out. Every time he'd tried it, Hawkins had flanked the bastard, flushed him out, and put him back on the trail to run.

Zane Lowe was dead, the last of the men Royce had brought to Denver. Travis had taken out the guy's central nervous system in an instant with a dead-on cranial cavity shot that was always messy, but also always effective, especially in a hostage situation. All those hours the Angel Boy spent up on the eighth floor in the armory had really paid off tonight. It had been a good call on Skeeter's part to bring the guy into the fold.

It had been a good call on General Grant's part to make sure SDF could take care of Royce once and for all. The man had cost them too much, and Hawkins had been keeping score.

Parts of Commerce City looked like Armageddon had come and gone: towering industrial buildings with harsh lighting and dark shadows, nothing green for miles or blocks in every direction, whole areas abandoned after the workday was done. Geiss Fasteners was on the edge of all that, and Royce had been going deeper into it every minute.

A sound from above had Hawkins glancing up in time to see a helicopter cut across the sky.

Shit. Nothing was ever easy, not in this line of work, but the people who did it didn't do it because they were looking for the least line of resistance. They resisted, always, with their very lives if need be.

Resisting hadn't been enough for Red Dog, though. *Fuck.* Even if she survived, there were no guarantees.

Old Royce, though, Hawkins was giving him an ironclad guarantee.

The man was running out of steam. A lot of assholes were going to be looking for work when he was dead, but given the state of the world, Hawkins didn't think they'd have any trouble finding it.

A flash of movement up ahead caught his eye. It was Royce all right, the only other living thing in the whole canyonlike landscape of refineries and factories. He was starting to double over a little, his feet dragging through the puddles that were only getting bigger the longer it rained. Lightning had flashed a few times, punctuated by great claps of thunder.

Royce's suit was sodden. Hawkins could see how it was pulling at the old guy, weighing him down. Royce's hair had thinned over the last two years, and every time lightning flashed, he could see the ex-agent's bald head gleaming in the light.

The man's whole crew had died in Commerce City in the last two hours, and Loretta had not been happy to hear it. But Grant had talked her into sending in her best cleanup crew, and by morning, it would be as if nothing had happened.

The only thing still needing to be done was killing Royce. Hawkins could have shot him half a dozen times, but he was running him instead, stalking him through the night.

Up ahead, the man stumbled, then slipped and fell to his hands and knees. He was still holding on to his pistol. When he didn't get up, Hawkins decided the night was over.

Raising his .45, he took careful aim and shot Royce precisely through the base of his skull. The ex-agent collapsed forward into a shallow, dirty puddle.

Royce was getting out of this life easy. Way too easy.

Hawkins walked over to him, kicked the gun away, holstered his firearm, and keyed his radio.

"It's done," he said.

CHAPTER
32

DAWN WAS BREAKING the sky when Honey heard the trucks pull up outside, the trucks taking Julia and Father Bartolo back into the mountains. She squeezed her sister's hand under the table, and Julia turned to her with a smile.

"Come on, Honey," she said. "Come pray with me."

It was the closing of the set piece that had become their good-byes since Malanca. Honey didn't try to talk her out of the choices she'd made, not anymore. She'd talked them both to death when Julia had first made her decision to join the church.

Rising from the table, Honey followed her into the sanctuary.

Peace, that's all her baby sister had wanted, and

no price had been too high to pay, certainly not giving up the York-Lytton life of empty society and jet-setting absurdities.

Empty to Julia. Absurd to Julia. Honey found meaning in her life, more than enough to sustain her, but she hadn't lost the man she'd loved to a cause she had to believe had been worthwhile, had to believe in with every cell of her being in order to accept the sacrifice that had been demanded.

They knelt at the altar, and Julia took her hand again.

Honey had never forgotten what Carl had looked like in that elevator. It had been carnage, with his blood all over Julia, and her sister screaming and screaming, helpless against the horror of what her privileged life had suddenly and shockingly become: an utter, senseless tragedy.

Honey had known exactly why that woman had been screaming out on the street next to the Palacio. The quality and tenor of the sound had cut through her like a knife, and for a few endless seconds it had all been too real again, Carl and Julia, and the men who had knocked Honey over racing out of the hotel, the assassins with black stockings over their faces and black guns in their hands. For an endless second, it had grabbed hold of her.

But Smith had been there, and he'd been more than enough.

"Hail, Mary, full of grace; the Lord is with thee," Julia began, her voice so young and sweet, like the curve of her cheek. So young. "Blessed art thou amongst women, and blessed is the fruit of thy womb."

"Holy Mary, Mother of God," Honey said with her. "Pray for us sinners."

HONEY watched until the last truck was out of sight. Four months, Julia had promised. She'd be leaving El Salvador in four months, and Honey could only hope she did. There had to be something out there better for her sister than a life of poverty and doing without even the barest trappings of civilization.

Sitting down on the front steps of St. Mary's, she brought the tail of the green parrot shirt to her face and pressed her nose into it, and hoped she could smell him. It was just a little bit crazy, but she thought maybe she could, and she could see where maybe she'd underestimated her reaction to him.

Time would tell. It always did.

Letting out a sigh, she looked back the way the trucks had gone. Sister Anna had promised her a ride back to her hotel. All the good nun had to do was contact her cousin, Roberto, who was going to contact his boss, Luis, who had a brother, who had a car she could hire.

It was going to be a bit of a wait. Fortunately, the stone steps of St. Mary's weren't too uncomfortable, even with her hurt butt. She could always go in and lie down in a pew, but it was nicer to be outside, with the sun rising, and a soft breeze blowing in from the ocean.

She let her gaze drift back to the street—and that's when she saw him, sitting on a bench under a stand of palm trees. He was very still, very relaxed, his feet square on the ground, his knees slightly apart, his hands folded together in his lap, and there wasn't a doubt in her mind that he was looking at her through those Ray-Bans.

The feeling that went through her was a hard one, a little too powerful, and it hit her all at once like a soft wave of recognition, that she could fall in love with him.

And why that should demoralize the crap out of her, she didn't know.

She watched him watching her across the quiet space of the empty churchyard and the deserted street. They were alone, with nothing but the wind and the sun between them and the night sliding away behind them.

She didn't know him. The truth was uppermost in her mind. But she knew what it meant when he unfolded his hands and beckoned to her. His palm was open and up, his fingers together, the gesture brief, self-assured, arrogant, and irresistible: *Come to me*.

Letting out a sigh and wondering if she had the strength to read him the riot act, she rose to her feet, pulled her tote close, and started down the steps.

GOD, what a lovely mess she was.

Smith let his gaze travel down the length of her, which didn't take long. There just wasn't that much of her, but what was there pleased him.

Her hips swayed with every step she took down the stone stairs of the church, one carefully placed foot at a time. He was impressed as hell that she'd gotten across San Luis on her own in the middle of the night, even more so in those shoes. They weren't quite as white as they'd been when he'd first seen her. The straps still worked and were buckled around her ankles, but one of the bows had lost its mooring.

She'd taken his clothes, which also pleased him, and whether she'd meant to or not, she'd left her ruined dress and those shamelessly sheer panties at the Palacio.

He was keeping the panties, a memento to go

with the gun she'd bought off the street—and yeah, he figured those two items pretty well summed up the night. He hoped he didn't dwell on it too much.

"You stole my pistol," he said when she was close enough to hear.

She'd slipped her big white sunglasses on while she crossed the street, and now deigned to push them down a little ways on her nose and flat-out knock him over with how green her eyes really were, in daylight, with the sun reflecting in them.

"It's heavy," she said, pushing the glasses back up and reaching in her tote to pull out the Sig.

She handed it over, and he checked the chamber, then slipped it into the holster at the small of his back, under his blue parrot shirt.

"The cabs are running one block over. I can get you out on a plane this morning, and in my professional capacity as your bodyguard, I highly recommend that you go. The party is going to start up all over again in a few hours. I can guarantee it." People had died in the night, so now there was revenge mixed in with the politics.

She looked up at him, and he could almost see the wheels churning, but not for long.

"Thank you," was all she said, and that was as it should be. He liked smart women. "What about you?"

He came. He went. He did the jobs he was paid to do.

"How are your feet holding up?" was all he said, gesturing up the street and waiting for her to start walking.

"Fine."

"Good. You had a big night. For a while there, I wasn't sure how you were doing." He looked over at her, but this close, mostly all he saw was the top of her head. Her hair was just too wild to see much beyond it. In sunlight, though, he could see the other ninety-nine shades of blond she had in it, and it was almost as if every curl was a different color—absolutely gorgeous.

"I've got luggage at the Royal Suites Hotel," she said, completely ignoring his thinly veiled accusation. He didn't blame her for that, but she had dumped him in the middle of the night, exfiltrated, left him behind when he'd committed to doing the job for her.

"Give me your address, and I'll have it sent." He pulled a small notebook and a mechanical pencil out of one of his cargo pockets.

She rattled off an address in Washington, D.C., a city he knew just well enough to know she was as rich as she looked if she lived in Adams-Morgan. Hell, even richer, considering that she was wearing his clothes.

But he wasn't going to dwell on that, either.

He did realize that somehow, almost inadvertently, he'd just gotten her address. If something came up, like with the panties or something, he guessed, at least now he could get ahold of her.

Yes, sir, that was him, not dwelling.

He could have found her anyway. He had her name, but it was nice that he'd gotten the address from her. It felt a little more personal than him investigating her, or siccing Skeeter on her.

"So how did it go with your sister?" He could be polite, even if she had dumped him and gone through his wallet. The signs had been unmistakable.

"Sad, like it always goes."

Well, that was definitely an opening.

"I have a little brother who gets into trouble all the time, too."

"Does he get into trucks at dawn with men carrying machine guns?"

"Actually, he does that quite a bit. He's a U.S. Army Ranger."

"Then he can take care of himself."

Yeah, he had to concede the point, just like he had to concede the point that he was really bad at this "morning after" chatter. If they could have just gone back to bed, he was sure they could have reached an understanding of what in the hell had happened last night—or at least he wouldn't be wondering about it so much.

But the girl did not look like she was in the mood.

He wasn't really either, not like instantly, but he could get there pretty quick.

"Do you want me to check your butt before you get on the plane?"

She looked at him over the tops of her sunglasses again, and if he wasn't mistaken, the littlest smile twitched the corner of her lips.

Score.

"I think my butt is fine."

"Thanks for the book. I'm really going to study it."

The smile was for real this time, curving both sides of her mouth.

God, she had a mouth—but he wasn't going to dwell on it.

When they reached the next street, his luck improved again. There was a cab. It only took a couple of minutes to get her inside and tell the driver where he wanted to go.

"Puede transportarnos a este lugar?" Could you transport us to this location? He showed the guy the map he kept in his wallet. It was always a handy thing to have, a map of the quickest way out

of Dodge, and more than once, having one had cut through a lot of confusion and saved his ass.

"*A la pista de aterrizaje?*" the driver asked, surprised. *To the airstrip?*

Smith understood. Tourists used the regular airport. Only the drug runners and the locals would have used the dirt airstrip—and guys like him.

"*Si. Tres kilometros nordeste.*" Smith knew what he wanted, and he wanted the airstrip three kilometers northeast of San Luis.

"*Bien,*" the driver said. *Good.* It was one of those deals where, if you knew where in the hell the airstrip was, you obviously knew what in the hell you were doing.

Close enough, Smith thought. He knew enough to get her out of San Luis.

By the time they hit the outskirts of town, he could tell she was starting to relax, and he understood. Her sister was long gone. There was no reason for Honoria York-Lytton to cool her little white platform heels in San Luis any longer. It was time to go home and forget how wild the night had gotten, forget being sad, and probably forget him.

He hated that last part. Truly, he did. He wasn't going to be forgetting her.

But the way she was ignoring him, so studiously keeping her gaze focused out the window, her back to him, made him wonder if she hadn't already wiped him off her memory banks. Then he noticed that as the palm trees and farmers' fields were flashing by on the side of the road, her shoulders were shaking.

She was crying.

Well, hell. He did the only thing he could. He reached for her, wrapping his hand around her upper arm and urging her to come closer.

She turned her head, and he saw the wet tracks of tears running down her cheeks, and in the next second she was in his arms.

Again. Thank God.

And her hands were on his chest, and her mouth was right there, and he kissed her, over and over and over, sweet and soft—and so it went, all the way to the airstrip. Just kissing. Lots of it. On her face, on his, sometimes with their mouths together. She licked his neck, and he almost told her licking wasn't fair, because there was no place for all the kissing to go, not in the backseat of a Salvadoran cab.

But he didn't say anything. It had been a crazy night, that was all, and kissing her was the right thing to do, right up until she was starting up the drop ramp to get into the plane, a twin-engine, low-wing Beech Baron.

"Take care of yourself, Honey." He kissed her

cheek one more time, while he held her in his arms one more time.

"You, too, Smith." She pressed her lips to the corner of his mouth, one more time, and he was pulling away and giving her a little push in the right direction, up the ramp. Honey York was going home, where she belonged.

But halfway to the hatch, she stopped and turned around.

"You never told me what the C stands for in C. Smith Rydell."

God, she was beautiful, with the sunlight in her hair and the sky behind her, with his pants rolled up to under her knees, and her shoes a testament to just how tough she'd been. A quarter of a million dollars—*geezus*, it was all a little unbelievable, that she'd done it and was getting out in one piece.

Oh, yeah, she was beautiful. More than beautiful, and he was never going to forget.

The C in C. Smith Rydell—a grin curved his mouth. She was a piece of work, all right.

"Next time," he said, giving her a short wave as he backed away.

Yeah. Next time.

CHAPTER

33

"I REMEMBER my mother," Gillian said from the middle of her hospital bed.

"Good."

"She's sweet."

"Very," Travis agreed. Lydia Shore was a very sweet woman, but maybe she was starting to hope too much, expect too much.

Gillian had survived the night in Commerce City, but the week since then had been full of ups and downs.

"I'm not sure about that guy she hangs with," Gillian said, then lowered her voice to a conspiratorial whisper. A small grin curved her lips. "I think she's doing him."

Travis grinned with her. "You mean that guy we

call your father?" His grin broadened. "Yeah, I think she's doing him, too."

A nurse came in then, and Travis stepped aside. It was something he'd been doing all week—stepping aside.

She was a hard woman, and she pushed him.

He heard Dr. Brandt come in, but he stayed at the window, looking out over the capital. Washington, D.C., wasn't such a bad city. He actually liked it, even if this time he hadn't gotten much beyond Walter Reed Medical Center.

Gillian had changed. Things were happening in her body and in her mind, and no one was placing any bets on how it was all going to turn out. She seemed to have gone to an entirely new level of strength and power and speed—and she remembered her mother.

Maybe that would help, Travis thought. Having something as sweet as memories of Lydia Shore in a person's brain had to be a help. Maybe inside that goddamn convoluted space called Red Dog's mind, Lydia could fight some of the battles that raged.

Royce was dead. Gillian knew it, and somehow, maybe, that was bringing her some peace.

Two days, that's how long she'd been physically comatose, while every machine they'd had hooked up to her had been going crazy, straight off the charts. Dr. Brandt had tracked every second of those days, charted them, studied them, been fascinated, and sometimes, secretly, Travis had wondered if the good doctor wasn't also just a little afraid—not *of* Gillian, but for her.

Then she'd "woken up," and the dark weight that had been crushing the life out of him had lifted.

Fuck.

She wanted to get back into the gym, back out on the range. She wanted to work. She wanted to run, and shoot, and probably to goddamn fly.

She was a hard woman.

"Angel?"

He turned at the sound of her voice. The nurse and Dr. Brandt had left, but probably not for long. Red Dog's hospital room was like Grand Central Station.

"Yeah, babe." He walked back over and sat down in a chair next to the bed.

She took his hand, which he didn't mind, and she leaned close, which he didn't mind too much. He'd been trying not to get too close.

"Want to help me escape?"

Two weeks ago, they would have done it together, made their escape, but now . . . but now he didn't know which end was the fuck up.

But she was close, and he was such a goddamn fool.

Leaning closer, he kissed her cheek, once,

lightly, then rose to his feet and went back to the window.

He couldn't do this.

"Angel."

"Don't," he said. "Just don't."

She tore him up, and sometime, someplace, at some goddamn moment, a guy had to cut his losses.

He knew now.

Dylan had been investigating a man named Sir Arthur Kendryk. The guy was actually an English lord, Lord Weymouth, and Travis knew now where Gillian had been that month when she'd fallen off the radar. Kendryk had been tied to the hit in Amsterdam. Apparently, he'd been after the same thing SDF had been tasked with acquiring: the death of a man, the shutting down of one path of terrorism that had threatened the United States and one of Kendryk's business deals.

Survival—they'd all been trained for it, trained to do whatever it took to survive.

Fuck.

He dragged his hand back through his hair and watched the cars driving by outside.

He had not been able to sort things out, and maybe he never would, not as long as he was with her.

"Travis?"

He hadn't heard her get out of bed and cross the

room, and now she was *way* closer than he thought he could bear, coming up behind him, wrapping her arms around him, sliding up under his arm.

He couldn't do this.

He started to unwrap her from around his waist, lifting her arms away, but she stopped him with a word.

"Please."

Yeah, that was a good word.

Please don't cheat on me.

Please don't lie to me.

Please don't—just fucking don't.

No doubt about it, please was a helluva word. He knew another helluva word, and with her way too damn close to do anything but remind him, he laid it out between them.

"Kendryk," he said, looking down and meeting her gaze straight on. She was his lover, yes, but she was also his partner, and she'd lied, by omission if nothing else. It was unacceptable.

And she knew it all, understood it all. Everything he was thinking was reflected in her golden-eyed gaze, along with a measure of regret that really didn't do a damn thing to make him feel better.

"A means to an end," she said—which also didn't do a goddamn thing to make him feel better.

"Bullshit," he said and looked back out the window. "You weren't that hard up for help." *You had me*, he wanted to say, and probably back her up against the wall and get in her face while he did it.

She'd had him, goddammit, and she'd known it. She'd known it from the start.

"I got hurt in Amsterdam. Kendryk's men found my position. They found me. He knew someone else was tracking his target, and he didn't want any interference, so he sent a team to take me out."

And they'd failed.

"How many were there?"

"Two in the first group. Four on the team that finally captured me."

Captured. His jaw hardened.

She'd been captured once before, by Negara and Souk and Royce—and they'd tortured her.

"You said you were hurt," he said, the deeper question implied.

"Roughed up during the initial fight. No other harm was done, not in the whole time I was there."

"Where?"

"I'm not sure. A castle in the woods. It could have been anywhere. I was released in London."

"And Kendryk?"

"I . . . I thought . . ." Her voice trailed off. After a moment, she let go of him and turned away. "I thought I could use him to get to Royce, and—"

"And you got used instead," he cut her off, his voice not nice. But *shit*. He didn't need to know the details, not from her. The thought of her being with another man was enough to make him sick, and nothing would change the facts.

"No." She shook her head, still faced away from him. "I got what I wanted. I got the Uzbek, and the Miami deal, and the rest of them, and now, because of what I did and how I did it, Royce is dead. It's just that—" She wrapped her arms around her middle, and suddenly she looked so alone, so singularly and frightfully alone. "It's just that the price is always high in this business. No matter how you try to cut your losses, you end up paying more than you want, no matter what you win, and every time, you tell yourself it was worth it anyway."

She was right, but that really didn't make him any less angry.

"It's all big boy rules out there," she continued, making a gesture toward the window and the densely packed metropolis of Washington, D.C. "There are no dispensations for being a girl, Angel, not in the work we do."

She was right again. He hated it, but she was right.

She lifted her shoulders in a small shrug, and he saw her wipe at her cheek with the back of her hand.

The gesture riveted him in place.

In two years, he hadn't seen her cry, ever. Red

Dog didn't cry. It was part of what she'd lost. It was in her charts and records, an emotional dysfunction.

"I'm stronger now than I was before," she said. "Not so desperate, not so willing to make sacrifices."

And you're crying, he thought, still held solidly in place.

"No matter what happens from here on out, I'll find another way, Travis. I won't give in to fear. Never again." She turned her head and looked up at him from over her shoulder.

And it had been fear motivating her, the morbid, self-destructive fear of Tony Royce, and of her own inconstancy, her own vulnerability, all the crap she couldn't control. He knew her better than anyone, and he knew that—and he was still so fucking blown up by the whole goddamn mess.

It would be so easy to throw it all away. To walk out the door and not look back, and just let the world know she'd done him wrong, the bad girl with the heart of steel.

So fucking easy.

And so impossibly hard.

So impossible.

He was tougher than that. Tougher than her.

Goddammit all anyway.

He looked at her where she was standing in

front of him, looked down at her "wind tunnel" hair and warm golden eyes, and he knew he was doomed.

Geezus. He hadn't known love could be so goddamn demoralizing.

She wasn't that big, that tall, but what she had was power. It pulsed through her in a steady, unending beat.

Thank God. It's what he needed to know. That she would go on.

"We're going to make it this time, right?" she asked, and he could tell by the tone of her voice that she wasn't at all sure.

But he was. This time.

"Yes." The answer was so simple, and right there in his heart. He hadn't had to go looking for it.

Because no matter what happened, he didn't want to live his days without this feeling, without the connection between them, the hot, dark sweetness of it running through him with every breath, of being part of her, of her being part of him.

Sliding his hand up around the back of her head, he gently pulled her in closer, bringing her against his chest. A sigh left her, and her arms tightened around his waist.

She was a hard woman, but that was good, because he was a hard man.

CHAPTER

34

"THIS COULD BE your worst idea ever," Gillian said, looking out over the crowd of professors, alumni, and benefactors of the University of Arizona filling up the ballroom of the exclusive Kittredge Mark Hotel on the outskirts of Phoenix.

"No," Travis disagreed. "I've definitely had worse."

"None involving me."

He grinned, without conceding anything.

"Come on," he said, directing her down the stairs to the main level. "This is therapy."

"This is nuts."

"Let me know if you recognize anybody."

Unlikely, she thought. Everyone looked alike, the whole crowd of people, the women in long dresses, the men in black-tie, the caterers in white, the small orchestra in red jackets and black pants. The colors were all different, the styles and shapes of their clothes, some more elegant than others, but the ease with which it all was worn looked the same: They belonged.

She did not.

Angel did.

No one wore a tuxedo with more style than Travis James, especially one of Dylan Hart's Armani tuxedos. He was by far the most outrageously handsome man in the room. He was also, without doubt, the deadliest, and yet nothing in his demeanor gave him away.

She felt exposed, like a walking advertisement for the killing arts. Nothing about her fit in with the people around her.

Everyone else looked satisfied, in their place, in their element, all of them buzzing around each other and the buffet tables laden with a dazzling assortment of food and lush bouquets of flowers. She did not "buzz," ever. She was always in stealth mode, a shadow, but it was damn hard to maintain that illusion dressed in red Versace and four-inch heels.

The event was fund-raising at its highest end, an auction for the benefit of the Environmental Sciences labs at the university, where she'd worked before she'd gone to Washington, D.C. and taken a job with General Grant. There were cruises to be had, one to Antarctica; lots of European travel; plasma televisions; lots of high-tech goodies; two automobiles, one with four-wheel drive; and one painting—a very large painting, which had been donated anonymously and sold for an outrageous amount of money and which would soon be hanging in its new home, on permanent display at the university.

Gillian wasn't sure what had compelled her to do it. Part of the healing process, Dr. Brandt had suggested, an honest gesture made in an effort to reach out and reclaim part of her past, but Gillian didn't think that was quite the reason behind her generosity.

She and Travis had toured the Environmental Sciences labs earlier in the day, along with the other benefit attendees, and nothing had sparked a memory, not the facility or any of the people, including a man named Ken, who had apparently been her husband at one point in time, before he'd left her for a very pregnant, blotchy-faced woman named Kimberly who had also not registered anywhere in Gillian's mind. Gillian had done her research before she'd come, and this was Ken and Kimberly's second child they were expecting. A lot of people had been on the tour, too many for either of them to easily approach her, but she'd known they were watching her, slightly confused, and wondering who she was, really.

She understood. She'd seen pictures of herself "before," and there was little left. Nothing in her bone structure had been altered, but without a certain softness in her face, without a certain air of scatterbrained preoccupation, there was no Gillian Pentycote. She was all Red Dog, from the top down.

And she'd donated a very expensive painting of her very naked boyfriend to her old university. She had some mental quirks, no one could deny it, and that was one of the quirkiest. She was sure the gesture was Freudian as hell.

"I know this is real important to Dr. Brandt, this whole retracing-my-life schtick, but . . ." She'd had enough.

"But we're moving on," Travis agreed.

She knew he understood. In the last few months, they'd visited just about every place Gillian Pentycote had ever been. But she was done. She had enough of her past to get by.

"And we're going to keep moving," she said.

"Work hard, work fast, babe."

"Stay low."

"Slow is smooth, and smooth is fast."

"Keep your powder dry."

"Yeah, that one, too." He grinned, then bent down and pressed a soft kiss to her face. "Here's to the future."

"That's where we're going, right, Angel?"

"Oh, yeah. You can count on it." He kissed her again, moving his mouth over her face, sliding his lips across her skin, holding her hand tight. "We're going into the future, baby . . . at light speed."

My heroes had the heart to lose their lives out on the limb
All I remember is thinking I want to be like them.
— "Crazy" by Gnarls Barkley

AUTHOR'S NOTE

Writing the CRAZY books has been a great ride from the minute I buckled into Jeanette the Jet and realized how much power and growl there could be in three hundred and eighty-three cubic inches of displacement hooked up to a pair of headers. Along the way, there have been some very talented and generous people in the shotgun seat.

My thanks and love go to Stan, as always, for being the bedrock. Thanks, also, to Nigel, who so kindly shared his encyclopedic knowledge about classic American muscle cars. Cindy Gerard—well, it's hard to adequately express what a huge impact she had on the books, from conception, inception, incubation, and making damn sure I toed the line. I owe her more than thanks. Rebecca flat-out deserves sainthood.

And then there are the wild boys and the gun diva—sometimes life hands us an unexpected gift. I got three when I walked into Colorado Gunworks wondering what it actually felt like to hold a pistol in your hand: Cullen "you had me at hello" Honeycutt, whose knowledge and generosity have been exceeded only by his kindness; the smokin' hot Tel Gallegos, gunpowder therapist extraordinaire; and Karl Kirov, who stopped by the shop one day and immediately started teaching me what I didn't know.

He's still at it.

All the mistakes in the books are mine, especially the one about the Glock in *Crazy Love*. As for Steele Street and SDF, look for more books about the chop-shop boys, beginning with *On the Loose*.

ABOUT THE AUTHOR

TARA JANZEN lives in Colorado with her husband, children, and two dogs, and is now at work on her next novel. Of the mind that love truly is what makes the world go 'round, she can be contacted at *www.tarajanzen.com*. Happy reading!

"Edgy, sexy and fast. Leaves you breathless!"
—JAYNE ANN KRENTZ

THE MISSION:

CRAZY HOT

TARA JANZEN

CRAZY HOT

ON SALE NOW

"Edgy, sexy and fast. Leaves you breathless!"
—Jayne Krentz

Regan McKinney, a studious paleontologist, isn't exactly accustomed to a life of high crime. But when a mysterious note from her missing grandfather leads her to a secret surveillance site maintained by a notorious special-ops task force, and headed by Quinn, a smoldering ex-fighter pilot, even Regan can't resist the chase.

Quinn was once on the fast track to a life of crime himself... until Regan's grandfather rescued him. Now Quinn owes it to them both to find the old guy. But throw in a deadly terrorist and some hot dinosaur bones, and a man could get himself killed... or fall crazy in love.

NOTHING MOVED in the shimmering heat.

Good God, Regan McKinney thought, staring over the top of her steering wheel at the most desolate, dust-blown, fly-bit excuse for a town she'd ever seen. The place looked deserted. She hadn't seen another car since she'd left the interstate near the Utah/Colorado border, and that had been a long, hot hour ago.

Cisco, the sign at the side of the road said, confirming her worst fear: She'd found the place she'd been looking for, and there wasn't a damn thing in it. Unless a person was willing to count a broken-down gas station with ancient, dried-out pumps, five run-down shacks with their windows blown out, and one dilapidated barn as "something."

She wasn't sure if she should or not. Neither was she sure she wanted to meet anybody who might be living in such a place, but that was exactly what she'd come to do: to find a man named Quinn Younger and drag him back to Boulder, Colorado.

Quinn Younger was the only lead she had left in her grandfather's disappearance, and if he knew anything, she was going to make damn sure he told the Boulder Police. The police never had believed that Dr. Wilson McKinney had disappeared. Since his retirement from the University of Colorado in Boulder, he'd made a habit of spending his summers moseying around the badlands of the western United States, and according to the results of their investigation, this year was no different.

But it was different. This year Wilson hadn't checked in with her from Vernal or Grand Junction, the way he always did, and he hadn't arrived in Casper, Wyoming, on schedule. She'd checked. It was true he was a bit absentminded, but he'd never gone two weeks without calling home, and he would never, ever have missed his speaking engagement at the Tate Museum in Casper.

Never.

THE MISSION:

CRAZY COOL

TARA JANZEN

CRAZY COOL

ON SALE NOW

"She's sizzling hot, he's icy cool . . . they're fire and ice, and crazy in love."

Thirteen years ago Christian Hawkins saved her life—only to spend two years in jail for a crime he didn't commit. Now it's déjà vu all over again when he rescues Kat Dekker from an explosion that rips through a Denver art auction. This time Christian plans on keeping a close eye on her until he figures out why somebody wants to kill her.

Kat hasn't forgotten the passionate summer nights in Christian's arms before everything went wrong. Now, the bullets are flying again and some-how Christian has become her sexy bodyguard. But staying out of danger is tough for two people who are this hot, crazy, and in love with each other.

"TWENTY BUCKS says the guy in the Armani suit is hired muscle."

Hired muscle? Katya Dekker looked up from her auction catalogue.

"Where?" She glanced around the outdoor amphitheater, her brow furrowing. She knew what her secretary, Alex Zheng, meant. She knew exactly what he meant, and she could only think of one reason for there to be any "hired muscle" at an art auction: her.

The thought only deepened her scowl.

She followed Alex's gaze across the delicately lit nighttime grounds of the Denver Botanic Gardens, searching through the crowd and the two dozen canopied tropical huts that had been erected for the dining comfort of the evening's guests. She found the "hired muscle" on the edge of a group of people next to the caterer's tent.

He was good, discreet, but she could spot a security detail at a hundred yards—and he had "high-priced bodyguard" written all over him, very high priced.

"What do you think of the suit?" Alex said. "I almost bought that one myself."

"No way, babe. Too structured. Too conservative," she told him, her gaze going over the man in the distance. There was nothing particularly remarkable about him, other than his choirboy looks, his shock of silky brown hair, and the alertness of his every move—the dead giveaway. He was quartering the gardens with his gaze, looking for God only knew what. Fund-raising art auctions hosted by the Denver Botanic Gardens were not hotbeds of intrigue.

Danger this hot
will break every rule of engagement.

THE MISSION:

CRAZY WILD

TARA JANZEN
Author of *Crazy Cool*

CRAZY WILD

ON SALE NOW

"Danger this hot will break every rule of engagement."

With her prim librarian looks, Cordelia "Cody" Stark doesn't look like a nuclear arms broker or the world's most dangerous woman, but nabbing her is Special Forces operative Creed Rivera's latest mission. That is, until a trio of thugs show up and he's forced to play hero...

Armed with secrets that could ignite a global inferno, Cody was already running out of places to hide—now a hotshot government agent has blown her cover. Trusting the hero who just saved her life is not an option, but resisting him is something else entirely. But when the bullets start to fly, a man and a woman running out of time are gearing up for the wildest adventure of their lives....

"TIMING IS going to be everything," Creed said, watching the two-and-a-half-ton truck grind its way up the switchbacks on the steep mountain road below them.

Next to him, Kid Chaos Chronopolous let out a short, humorless laugh.

Creed lowered the binoculars and wiped the back of his hand across his mouth. Behind them, the sun was setting on the high peaks of the Peruvian Andes. A light mist of rain turning to snow filled the air.

That was fine with Creed. He preferred his revenge cold.

They'd been in Peru for three weeks, traveling the desolate backcountry of the Cordillera range, roughing it out of an old army Jeep with no windshield, no doors, and no roof—waiting for Castano and Garcia to make a run for Puerto Blanco, the rebels' last refuge.

They weren't going to make it.

Kid reached for the binoculars and set them to his eyes. "Two guys in the cab."

"Castano riding shotgun," Creed said, pulling his black stocking cap lower on his head, then reaching around and tying his hair back at the base of his neck.

"Garcia at the wheel," Kid confirmed. He was unshaven, his skin burned brown by the sun, his dark hair long and shaggy from his months on the trail. He and Creed had chased Castano and Garcia from the jungles of Colombia and across the fetid swamps of the Amazon, like hounds on the scent, down the length of Peru.

But this is where it ended, here in the wild mountains in the wind and the snow.

THE MISSION:

CRAZY KISSES

You can't turn
down the heat
on a mission
this hot....

CRAZY KISSES

ON SALE NOW

"You can't turn down the heat on a mission this hot."

Professional soldier Kid Chronopolous moves in stealth and shadow to take out the world's deadliest threats. After barely surviving a hair-raising mission in South America, Kid comes home to Panama City for some R & R . . . and finds a bikini bottom that can belong to only one woman.

Nikki McKinney has never forgiven Kid for vanishing from her life after the mind-blowing passion they shared. Now he's back, as she's rising to the top of the local art scene. But her safe, sheltered world is about to be rocked. There's a bounty on Kid's head—and his enemies don't care if they take him dead or alive. With dangerous people gunning for him, Kid's got Nikki running for cover . . . and right into his arms. Keeping her safe is his latest mission. Keeping their hands off each other is out of the question . . .

THERE WAS a bikini bottom in his bathroom.

Curious as hell, Kid picked the tiny scrap of green-and-purple cotton up off the towel bar and turned it over in his hand.

It wasn't unusual for him to come home and find somebody crashing at his place. He'd known the instant he walked in that someone was there. The house in Panama City had belonged to his brother, and J.T. had always had an open-door policy.

But the bikini bottom was unusual.

Combat boots, surfboards, cases of beer—that's what he usually found. Not outrageously green bikini bottoms with purple palm fronds printed on them.

It was enough to make a guy think.

About sex.

And about death.

He swore softly and put the swimsuit back on the towel bar. J.T. had been the kind of guy who took care of people, a lot of people. Some of them had been women—mostly friends, but a couple of ex-lovers had shown up over the last few months. Kid didn't think he could face one of them tonight, and have to be the one to tell them J.T. was dead. He still felt about half dead himself.

Protect. Defend. Resist.
Giving in to temptation has never been more dangerous.

THE MISSION:

CRAZY LOVE

TARA JANZEN

CRAZY LOVE
ON SALE NOW

"Protect. Defend. Resist. Giving in to temptation has never been more dangerous."

Government operative Dylan Hart has survived some of the riskiest missions known to man. But no nemesis could have prepared the Special Defense Forces commander for the newest member of his team Skeeter Bang. A street-smart, leather-clad heartbreaker, Skeeter has been recruited to aid Dylan's latest mission: steal a top-secret file and bury it before all hell breaks loose.

Teaming up with a man who may be the last bona fide defender of the free world is a risk Skeeter's ready to take—until a black-tie Washington soiree erupts in a bullet-flying free-for-all. Now Skeeter's got danger on her trail and Dylan arousing every bad-boy fantasy she ever had. Being in the wrong place at the wrong time is about to plunge one man and woman right into the sizzling line of fire. . . .

PINK.

Sweater.

Short.

Skirt.

Long.

Legs.

Dylan Hart flipped his cell phone shut and rubbed his hand over his forehead, trying not to stare at the girl on the other side of the office. She was out to slay him, his nemesis, the bane of his existence—Skeeter Bang, five feet eight inches of blond bombshell leaning over a computer.

Jail.

Bait.

She knocked a cigarette out of the pack of Mexican Faros on the desk and struck a match off her belt.

"Put that out," he ordered. She knew there was no smoking in the office.

"Make me," she said, then stuck the Faro between her lips and inhaled, holding the match to the end of the cigarette. A billow of smoke came out of her mouth when she exhaled.

Make me?

Dylan was the boss of 738 Steele Street in Denver, Colorado, second in command of Special Defense Force, SDF, a group of tough-as-nails black ops shadow warriors who specialized in doing the Department of Defense's dirty work.

Make me?

"Put out the damn cigarette, Skeeter," the man working at the last computer said. "And if you bend over that desk one more time, I'm going to paddle you."